BEYOND
BELIEF

ALSO BY HELEN SMITH

Alison Wonderland
Being Light
The Miracle Inspector

OTHER TITLES IN
THE EMILY CASTLES SERIES

Three Sisters
Showstoppers
Invitation to Die

BEYOND BELIEF

Helen Smith

THOMAS & MERCER

Text copyright © 2014 Helen Smith
All rights reserved.

Published by Thomas & Mercer, Seattle

www.apub.com

ISBN-13: 9781477849729
ISBN-10: 1477849726

Cover design by Scott Barrie

Library of Congress Number: 2013945214

Printed in the United States of America

For my parents

CHAPTER ONE

THE EXPLORATION OF
SCIENCE AND CULTURE

It was a Thursday evening in March; the sky had given up its nightly fight against the dark a little later than the day before, but it still felt more like winter than spring. Twenty-six-year-old Emily Castles stepped out of the darkness into the headquarters of the Royal Society for the Exploration of Science and Culture, not far from Buckingham Palace in London. She was tired, poor, bored and hungry. In the space of an hour, at least one of those conditions would be relieved.

Emily had an appointment in the boardroom. A uniformed doorman escorted her there along a wide corridor with a marble floor, past stuccos and painted frescos, past the opulent and imaginatively stocked members' bar and the walnut-paneled library. When they reached the heavy wooden door to the boardroom, the doorman knocked and Emily went in. The walls of the boardroom were decorated with emerald silk wallpaper and portraits of past presidents. Motes of dust danced in the light of the tall brass lamps that stood at the corners of the room. At the far side of a polished expanse of a wooden table sat Gerald Ayode, current president of the society, beneath an unflattering oil painting of himself.

Studying the portraits, Emily was treated to a pictorial time line of the changing face of the society, as represented by its presidents. In the nineteenth century, when the society had been founded, all the presidents had been moustachioed white men. Emily imagined them holding furious discussions about the weight and location of the soul, the best way to document the existence or otherwise of fairies, the size and number of angels, and the likely date that the first British man would travel to the moon. In the late twentieth century, when much of the exploration would have turned to mapping the mind and understanding how it might be used to investigate the spiritual realm as well as control the physical, two of the presidents had been severe-looking white women. Now, in the twenty-first century, the current president of the Royal Society for the Exploration of Science and Culture was a large, pleasant-looking black man.

Gerald was wearing a charcoal-gray suit and an anxious expression, his short black hair threaded with more silver than when he had first taken up office. His hands rested protectively on a buff-colored folder on the polished wooden table in front of him.

Next to Gerald sat a woman known professionally as Perspicacious Peg. She was a big woman in her fifties with a round face and muddy-blonde, wavy hair cut short in a no-nonsense style. She was wearing a paisley shawl draped over one shoulder, as if she expected to be handed a colicky baby to wind, and wanted to protect her clothes in case it should bring up its feed. Next to Peg sat Dr. Muriel Crowther, a philosophy professor who lived across the street from Emily Castles in Brixton, South London. It was she who had summoned Emily here.

Emily was a bright young woman who had spent the last two weeks working on a temporary assignment in a small, stuffy office just off the Strand, typing up interview notes for an executive recruitment agency. Though the answers given by the candidates had sometimes been creative, Emily's work had not. In fact, it had been stultifying. Emily had never quite found a job that suited her, a boyfriend who was clever enough for her, or a home that was close enough to the center of London to make the commute to work tolerable. But because she was young, that was OK. She was still at the age where she was moving toward possibilities, rather than away from them.

That Thursday evening, Emily had been planning to go home, have a nice hot bath and a cup of tea, eat something cheap and wholesome, like a baked potato, then lie on the sofa watching undemanding programs on TV. She'd had a miserable day. But then came Dr. Muriel's whispered phone call: "Can you meet me tonight, Emily? I need your help to investigate a suspicious death." So Emily had come to the society's headquarters straight from work, walking past St. James's Park and partway along the Mall toward Buckingham Palace, before turning off to reach the quiet street where the white-fronted Regency building was located. She reflected that if she came to work here every day, she could walk through St. James's Park in the morning, across the little bridge over the lake and past the pelicans, past the tourists photographing themselves feeding the squirrels, into Horse Guards Parade and past the sentries on horseback. There would always be some joy in a walk that took that route to work. But the people sitting in front of her now didn't look joyful. They were solemn and anxious.

"Gerald Ayode," said Dr. Muriel, introducing her companions, "and Perspicacious Peg."

"Just 'Peg' is fine," said Peg, amiably. Emily recognized her as a self-professed psychic who had a column in a Sunday newspaper. She had been a regular guest on breakfast TV about ten or fifteen years ago. Now her weekly "horrorscopes" in the *Sunday Sentinel*, which dwelt on all the bad things that might happen to the reader in the ensuing seven days, were hugely popular among young media folk for their campily dire predictions. If Peg's readers got to the end of the week without any of the bad things happening, it was a cause for celebration, i.e., an excuse to get drunk on a Friday night. Emily wasn't a hipster. At the end of the week she looked forward to treating herself with tea and television rather than a skinful of drink. But even she had read the horrorscopes.

"I'm Emily," said Emily, sitting down.

"You're the psychic investigator?" asked Gerald.

"No."

"But you have a dog?"

What on earth had Dr. Muriel told them? "I'm afraid my dog's dead."

"Ah." Peg seemed reassured. "So that's it."

"Who's died?" Emily asked.

Gerald wrinkled his nose and looked offended, as if Emily was suggesting there was a horrible odor in the room.

"No one . . . yet," said Dr. Muriel. "I think we should give you some background. Gerald's chairing a conference that's taking place in Torquay this weekend."

"Belief and Beyond," said Gerald. "You might have heard about it?"

Emily hadn't.

"Philosophers, psychologists, anthropologists, ethicists and theologians gather to debate the nature of belief," said Dr. Muriel. "I go every year. It's great fun."

"Muriel's acted as my advisor in programming the academics," Gerald said. "And this year, as we'll be joined for the first time by mediums, hypnotists and psychics, Peg has acted as my advisor in programming *them*. At this conference we . . . we'll try to find common ground. We'll talk about *why* we believe what we believe, not whether it's right or wrong." Gerald glanced toward Peg. "We'll try not to say, 'I have the answers, and you do not.'"

"Unless there's a book to sell," said Dr. Muriel cheerfully. "Then the gloves are off."

"The exploration of science and the exploration of culture," said Gerald. "That's what it's all about. That's what this society's all about. And this year's conference will be bigger and better than ever."

Peg folded her arms and sat back in her chair. "Culture's what it's called nowadays when people believe what scientists don't understand."

"We used to be the Royal Society of Science and Spiritualism," Gerald told Emily. "Had to change the name back in the 1920s when there was all that to-do about people seeing fairies."

Emily was so tired and hungry, before too long she'd be seeing fairies instead of dust dancing in the light from the brass lamps. She wanted to get home to her baked potato. "I'm not sure why you need me?"

"We need a future crimes investigator," said Dr. Muriel, with a mischievous smile.

"Well . . ." said Gerald. He held up his hands in front of him, palms forward, as if trying to hold back these absurdities.

"I've had a premonition, but the police won't take it serious. You know what they're like with people like us." Peg spoke with the dignity of the oppressed, enunciating her words carefully in her London accent, as if she suspected the ghosts of the past presidents were lined up behind their portraits, ready to leap out and judge her for the accent, even if they didn't object to the colloquialisms. "They're a bunch of fuddy-duddies at Scotland Yard. In America they're more open minded. Missing person, kidnap, site of a shallow grave in a forest, they'll listen to a psychic. And I *have* called in to American radio programs on the subject over the years, and my contributions *have* been warmly received, and I *have* conveyed my thoughts and impressions of one or two high-level cases to police officers in America—and been treated with respect. Over here, you call the police to tell them you got a message from the other side, you hear them sniggering before they put the phone down."

"You called them today?" Emily asked her.

"I told them I'd had a premonition that someone would die in Torquay this weekend. And the person on the end of the phone actually says to me, 'Madam, we don't have a future crimes unit.' The cheek of it!"

"And this premonition was connected to one of your . . . hor-rorscopes?" Emily tried to sound polite.

"Not the horrorscopes, dear. That's entertainment, for the news-papers. Pure tongue-in-cheek. If you can't have a laugh then what's the point of getting up in the morning? That's what I always say. But I take very serious my mediumship and my telepathic skills. I've had numerous very alarming messages."

"What's going to happen exactly?"

"Well, I don't know *exactly*."

"I see."

"I'm getting a gentleman choking, gasping for breath."

That wasn't much to go on. Strangled? Poisoned? Hanged? Asthma attack? A large lump of food gone down the wrong way?

"It's something to do with water. He's drowning, Emily."

"Who is it? Do you know?"

Peg removed the buff-colored folder from under Gerald's hands and slid it across the table to Emily. "Have a look at this."

Emily hesitated for just a moment before opening it. What would she see? How would she feel looking into the drowned eyes of someone who wasn't yet dead?

Inside there was a glossy poster, which Emily unfolded like a map and laid on the table in front of her, standing up to get a better look at it. It was illustrated with a photograph taken at the seaside. A man aged about thirty, wearing the traditional stage magician's garb of top hat and a red-lined black cape, stood several yards out beyond the shoreline, out where the sea would be deeper than the height of a man. He was facing the shore. His feet skimmed the top of the water, his arms were outstretched. Behind him, the waves rushed toward a pinkish horizon where the sun had just set. His expression was arrogant—mocking, even. His gaze was intense; full of life.

Emily read the words printed across the poster in white lettering:

BEYOND BELIEF?

TORQUAY
29–31 MARCH 2013

BELIEFANDBEYOND.CO.UK
#BELIEFANDBEYOND

"Edmund Zenon," said Gerald.

"A provocative picture for Easter weekend, isn't it?" said Dr. Muriel. "The Christ-like pose, with arms outstretched."

"He's offering fifty thousand pounds to anyone who can prove the existence of the paranormal this weekend," Peg told Emily.

"For a TV show? Like *Britain's Got Talent* or something?"

"No, no!" Gerald smiled at the idea. "It's a serious scientific study. All participants vetted beforehand, all of them members of professional organizations, like the Association of Psychics, Paranormals and Spiritualists. Think of the security issues if we let just anyone show up!"

Peg wasn't smiling. "I wish he hadn't offered the money, Gerald. It's tacky. Makes it into a form of entertainment."

"So he didn't tell you he was going to offer the money when you invited him?" Emily asked her.

"I didn't invite him. Gerald did. Me and Edmund Zenon don't see eye to eye, so to speak. He's a well-known skeptic. A rationalist.

Call it what you want, he doesn't believe in the paranormal, so how does he think anyone's going to prove it exists, in Torquay of all places, this weekend?"

"It's not that he doesn't *believe*," Gerald corrected her. "He merely states that it has yet to be proved. We're fortunate he agreed to join us in Torquay," he told Emily. "With all his recent television appearances and the sold-out Don't Believe the Hype tour to promote his new book, he's a celebrity. He'll bring a lot of much-needed attention to the work of the society, of which the conference is a small but important element."

Peg scrunched up her face and worked her tongue around inside her mouth, as if a filling had come loose. But she said nothing.

Gerald tapped at the poster, impressed by Edmund's celebrity. "This image was projected onto the outside of the Royal Festival Hall when he did his gig there last week!"

"Could the image have triggered the premonition?" Emily suggested to Peg. "The picture of the magician standing on the water put the thought of drowning into your head?"

"I know the difference between a psychic vision and a daydream. If my head got filled with nonsense every time I walked past a poster with a striking image on it, I'd be having premonitions about holidays in Egypt and Marks & Spencer ready meals."

"Well—" Emily wanted to be conciliatory. But Peg wasn't quite finished.

"And footballers in their underpants."

Emily had been standing to examine the poster. Now she returned to her chair. "Well, if the police won't listen, have you tried contacting Edmund directly?"

"I've put a call into his management agency to ask them to pass on a message." Peg glared at Gerald. "*You* should call him. Tell him to cancel. Is it worth it, just for the publicity?"

"Not if he's going to die," said Emily.

"It may not be him," said Gerald.

Peg beckoned for Emily to hand her the poster. Emily slid it back across the table. Peg passed her hands above it as if she was trying to detect warmth from it. The movement was fairly brisk, at about the speed of someone scanning an item at the self-service till in a supermarket. Then she withdrew her hands and adjusted her sleeves, calm and professional: a veterinary surgeon who has been up to the elbow examining a cow in calf. "When you get a premonition, you don't see it clearly. It's not like watching the television. You'd be lucky to see a face or hear a name. You get clues and you interpret the information. That's the skill."

"Like a cryptic crossword," said Gerald.

"Or a game of charades," said Dr. Muriel.

Emily ignored them and talked to Peg. "But you think the drowning man is Edmund Zenon?"

Peg sighed. "It could be anyone. Could be *you*, Gerald."

Gerald smiled bravely.

"I'm in touch with my network of psychics up and down the country and I'll tell you something for nothing, Emily: the forums are buzzing, emails going back and forth. Some say they can see a woman drowning. Some say it's a man. But Edmund Zenon's haunting a lot of people's dreams. Now, I know what you're going to say."

Emily wasn't sure what she was going to say. She waited for Peg to tell her.

"You're thinking, 'If something's been foreseen, then surely it can't be changed.' Common misconception." Peg spoke kindly. "Future events *can* be influenced with enough positive energy sent in their direction. You know the Leaning Tower of Pisa has stopped tilting? Have you ever asked yourself how that happened?"

Emily admitted she hadn't.

"Strong, invisible arms keep it up, most of them belonging to women. And Neil Armstrong may have been the first man on the moon, fair enough. But he walked hand in hand up there with a circle of strong-minded, spiritual women."

"There were women on the moon before Neil Armstrong?"

"Not literally. Not physically. The women were down here helping him. We can fly to the moon or visit the pyramids when we open our minds to the spirit world. My new book, *Psychic Techniques for Future Positivity*, can give you all the information you need. I'll have some copies with me in Torquay."

"And you want me to use these techniques to try and stop Edmund Zenon getting killed?"

"No, dear! We'd never give an assignment like that to an amateur."

"What, then?"

Gerald pointed across the room to a portrait of a pale woman with an oblong face, her eyelids half-closed and unfocussed, as if she was trying to see beyond what was immediately in front of her, to connect with a more spiritual dimension. Or perhaps, thought Emily, she had been brought here straight from work at dinnertime, and she was close to fainting because she was so desperately hungry?

"Lady Lacey Carmichael, president of this society from 1935 to 1939," said Gerald. "Her husband and brothers were killed in the First World War. She was a woman of great sadness . . . and great wealth. After the First World War, she became a pacifist and a vegetarian, with an interest in spiritualism. In the events leading up to the outbreak of the Second World War in 1939, she stepped down from the office of president to campaign for world peace. She vowed to continue her campaign even after she died, declaring that if she heard news of an impending tragedy, she would try to communicate with the society to warn us about it from the other side. She left a password that she would use, if she ever got through—no one knows it except the president of the society. It's passed on as part of the inauguration ceremony."

Emily gawped a bit at this. "You think Lady Lacey's been communicating with Peg about World War Three?"

"Well, no."

"But she's transmitted the password?"

"No, dear," said Peg.

"Lady Lacey has never succeeded in contacting anyone, unfortunately," Gerald admitted. "But she left some funding as part of a legacy, you see, so that we could investigate fully if a message should get through to us from the other side, no matter who it's from. As Peg is working with the society to advise us on the conference, I believe her premonition qualifies as being worthy of investigation. Anyway, I've checked with our lawyers and they've allowed access to the funds. So we'd like you to investigate and write a report about the premonition and its outcome."

Emily appealed to Dr. Muriel. "Couldn't one of your students do it?"

It was Gerald who responded. "No, it has to be someone . . . sensitive. Lady Lacey was quite particular about that. Muriel told us about your connection to your dog, Jessie. It makes you a suitable candidate."

Dr. Muriel beamed.

"But I don't . . . I don't *connect* with Jessie. I just think about her now and again. I felt very sad when she died, but I'm over it now. She's not my spirit guide!"

"You haven't developed your sensitivities yet, dear," said Peg. "But you've got the right aura." She turned to Gerald. "She'll pass."

"Even if I don't believe in it?" Emily was incredulous.

"It's your observational skills I'm interested in," said Gerald, "rather than your aura."

"We'll see if we can get you involved in some nurturing circles, Emily," said Peg generously. "I must give you my card. If you're interested, I can help you develop your skills when we get back from Torquay next week. I do one-to-one or group sessions, depending on your spiritual needs and your financial situation."

Gerald pressed on. "Muriel said you're a vegetarian? That was something else Lady Lacey was quite keen on."

"She is." Dr. Muriel smiled proudly.

Gerald had saved the best for last. "And are you on Twitter?"

Emily shook her head. *Twitter?*

"Well, never mind." Gerald looked disappointed. "Lady Lacey didn't include any stipulations about that—it's something I'm keen on myself. We're leaving for Torquay tomorrow. I take it you're not working as it's Good Friday? I'd be delighted if you would join us for Belief and Beyond."

"I was going to spend the weekend in my garden."

Gerald leaned forward and spoke persuasively. He taught part-time at a university and he was used to dealing with impoverished young people who dined too often on baked potato.

"We will, of course, pay your accommodation, meals and modest expenses. What do you say? Shall I book you a ticket for the train to Torquay with Muriel tomorrow?"

"A weekend by the seaside," said Dr. Muriel. "Fresh air and palm trees. A couple of nights in a fancy hotel."

"You want me to investigate a suspicious death that hasn't happened yet, using a legacy from a long-dead member of the British aristocracy—and the main reason you've decided to hire me is because I have a dead dog and I'm vegetarian?"

"And because you carry a notebook." Dr. Muriel grinned at Emily. "That'll come in *very* useful for gathering material for the report."

"We'll pay you four hundred pounds," said Gerald.

"Five hundred," said Dr. Muriel. "Plus expenses."

Gerald only paused for a moment. "Five hundred, then. What do you say, Emily?"

It was a more appealing way to earn money than spending her days in a dingy basement in an office in London, typing up lies. "All right, then. I'll go to Torquay with you tomorrow. The forecast isn't very good for the weekend. I can start work on my garden next Saturday."

Gerald stood and leaned over the table to shake Emily's hand. "We could get you set up on Twitter."

"I'm quite a private person."

"We have a hashtag, you see." Gerald switched the poster round again so it faced Emily, and he pointed to the string of letters underneath the picture: #BELIEFANDBEYOND.

"Hashtag," Dr. Muriel said appreciatively, as she unhooked the silver-topped cane she always carried from the back of her chair. "Sounds like something you'd have deep-fried and served with chili sauce on a road trip in America."

Gerald spoke earnestly. "A hashtag is an Internet search term, Muriel. It will help people to find us online and get updates on the conference. What are we thinking at any given moment of the day? Hmm? If we wish to modernize, we need to let people know! Transparency, that's the key to success in business these days. And the society, despite its royal charter and long, eminent history, is a business like any other. We need sponsorship if we're to survive. And the best way for sponsors to find us is through social media. If we can get you set up, you can Tweet your thoughts from Torquay, Emily. It's instantaneous; spontaneous. Very exciting."

"I'm not spontaneous. I like to think things over," said Emily apologetically. "That's why I carry a notebook."

"Oh my days!" Peg remained in her seat, arms folded, as Emily and Dr. Muriel made their way toward the door. But she looked pleased. "She knows her own mind, this one. See you tomorrow, Emily."

Emily and Dr. Muriel planned to travel back to Brixton together. As they reached the Mall, Dr. Muriel stepped off the pavement, waving her cane. Then she put thumb and forefinger in her mouth and whistled at an advancing black taxi. The taxi had already started to slow down so the whistle was unnecessary, but its ferocity impressed Emily and made her giggle. Dr. Muriel gave the driver the name of the street where they lived in Brixton, then she stepped aboard, cane tucked under her arm, like a general about to be driven to the front to inspect her troops.

Emily pulled the door shut behind her and settled into the backseat next to her friend. The taxi turned and doubled back up the Mall, passed Buckingham Palace, then headed south across the Thames into the chilly late-winter darkness toward Brixton.

Crossing the Thames at night, with the bridges all lit up, was one of Emily's private joys. London seemed alive then, a glittering dragon whose protection could be claimed by whoever gazed on it and admired it, though it would never be tamed by anyone.

She wondered if Dr. Muriel was thinking the same. But her friend was thinking about Twitter. "There's very little attraction in it for academics. One becomes an academic in order to grandstand. One wants to publish papers that are twenty thousand words long. One wants to hold the attention of enraptured students and fellow professionals for hours at a time. Think of an idea as taking the shape of a coconut. You're visualizing something like a hard, little hairy head. Yes?"

Emily nodded.

"It's the job of someone like me who thinks for a living to get inside at the precious sweet meat of it and hand it about so people can feast on it. Think of me, Emily, as the person at the fairground with three balls in her hand, trying to knock that coconut off its stand and claim my prize."

Emily did as she was bid, though she had to make an effort not to giggle.

"Twitter acts a sort of grater, you see, shaving the edges off the delicious sweet meat and sprinkling a few dry wisps of it online. What sort of a feast is that? Being enigmatic is fine. But if I wanted to write haiku, I'd have become a poet, not a philosopher."

"I'm not on Twitter, so I haven't really got an opinion on it."

Now Dr. Muriel tried to hide her amusement. "If we restricted our opinions to matters of which we have direct experience, the world would soon be a dull place."

But things were never dull when Emily was with Dr. Muriel. It was one of the reasons she had agreed to go to Torquay. That and the five hundred pounds.

When they reached Brixton, Dr. Muriel and Emily were deposited in the quiet street where they lived opposite each other. There, in their separate residences—Emily in her ground-floor garden flat, Dr. Muriel in her larger red-brick house—they had the last night of untroubled sleep they would enjoy for a while.

CHAPTER TWO

GONE

Sarah and Tim Taylor were in their sitting room in Northampton with Joseph Seppardi, talking about the future. This was slightly unusual for Joseph. Generally his clients wanted to talk about the past.

"We have to stand up for what we believe," said Sarah. She was a sturdy woman with graying blonde hair that looked as if someone had hacked at it with a pair of shears. She was a keen gardener, and not vain about her appearance, so it was possible that one day last week, or the week before that, she had pruned a rambling rose or the branches of an apple tree with a pair of shears and then turned the instrument on herself. When she was younger she'd had an English rose appearance, with pale skin and a soft blush to her cheeks. Now the capillaries under the skin on her cheeks were broken and red, the clusters of delicate colorful lines resembling some other plant in her garden—a geranium, perhaps.

Tim, her husband, had managed to hold on to a few things in his life. His hair was one of them. Sarah was another, of course. Till death do us part. His job, his house, his friends at the golf club; everything else seemed lost. He had realized his sense of fair play was gone not long after Liam had gone. Gone, gone, gone, gone, gone, gone, gone. That horrible, mournful, wicked word that sounded like the clang of a funeral bell and meant he had been left behind and had to get on with it. And then along came Joe. The Restoration Man, Tim called him, because of what he had restored to them. Being English, you had to make a joke of it, even death. Even your son's death.

16

Tim was still English. He ought to remember to add it to the list of things that hadn't gone, when he enumerated them, as he sometimes did. He'd only had one son—one child—now he had none. He had been a father and couldn't un-be a father. But it was difficult to hold on to what it meant now that his son was gone. Gone. So he played up to the other roles that had been assigned him in life, to help to hold onto those. Husband, employee, friend, Englishman.

You get past forty and—Tim was pretty certain of this because he had watched his father and other men go past this age—you're not meant to learn new things. It's all you can do to try not to forget. Where did I put my socks, my glasses, my keys? My son. Where did I put my son? I put him in a coffin and then he was gone.

Now Tim had a new role. He was a believer. He wasn't sure, if he was going to be absolutely honest (and he had no intention of being absolutely honest with Sarah), that he did believe in it. Still, he had been cast in the role of believer by his wife. Seeing her survive each day had been what had saved him, rather than the messages from Liam. The messages had been trivial to the point of being annoying. But they comforted Sarah. Joseph Seppardi had restored Liam to them. And that meant that when Tim woke up and remembered and looked at his wife, she was still here, even though at the beginning she had said she couldn't bear to be.

Tim and Sarah were nice. That's how people described them. They were decent people who had survived the loss of their son. No one should have to bury a child; it was a common sentiment, often expressed. Actually Liam had been cremated and his ashes had been scattered in a favorite place. But that was hardly the point.

"You did right," Liam had said afterward. "You did what I would have wanted. You did the right thing." He had been a typical monosyllabic teenager, preoccupied with teenage boy things, too old to climb onto Sarah's lap and give her a cuddle. She had missed that, with him growing up. Liam had been a sweet child, then a mischievous toddler, then a sporty boy, then a tall, awkward, slightly secretive teenager. His father was tall. Like his father, no doubt Liam would have grown out of the awkward stage and grown up to be a nice man. Would have. Should have.

Sarah now sometimes thought how lovely it would have been to keep hold of Liam if he had survived, however badly incapacitated and uncommunicative. The one-sided chats and cuddles. The never growing up and leaving you. Sitting at his bedside, holding his hand, confiding in him. Talking about his father, maybe, about things she might not even have told a woman friend. She thought sometimes that it would be *nice* to have Liam here, even with his back broken and half his head hewn off. That's because she didn't know what it was like to tend a severely injured young man. She only knew what it was like to tend his spirit.

She was preoccupied with something else now: she had been provoked and she would have her fight. This man called Joseph Seppardi had given comfort to her, had spent hours and hours helping her through her grief. Now he and others like him needed her help. She would go with him to the seaside town of Torquay—and Tim would go with her, of course—and when she got there she was going to do whatever it took to help Joseph. She would be as tireless and tenacious as Joseph had been when getting the answers Tim and Sarah had wanted in their grief.

Sometimes Sarah thought she'd relish a real fight rather than what people called a fight these days, which was little more than an argument. A fight to the death, and if her life should be taken, so much the better. She'd be reunited with Liam, he'd be whole again, according to Joseph Seppardi, and she in her prime, around thirty years old, both of them closer in age than they had ever been, and closer emotionally. And if, during the course of such a fight, she ended up taking a life rather than giving hers? That would be OK. Sarah would gladly take one life to save many others if needs be. It would be an easy decision to make.

"We have to stand up for what we believe," Sarah said now. "That magician wants to make a mockery of people like us. If he had his way, people like Joseph would never be able to help the bereaved. We have to do something."

Sarah was one of those ordinary women who can be formidable fighters when provoked into doing the right thing. She wouldn't fight for herself but she'd fight for others. She hadn't been able to fight to keep Liam alive. He was dead or dying when they got to him. They had said—Liam always said—he felt no pain, that it was instant. (Tim wasn't so sure. Even the dead must sometimes deceive. Even a dead boy might lie if it meant doing a kindness for his mother.)

But now Sarah was going to fight and so Tim was going to stand up for, well, for what Joseph and Sarah believed. He was going to stand by Joseph. At the beginning, when he'd heard what had happened to Liam, Tim had just wanted to lie down and die. Standing was better. Standing up, standing by: any kind of standing, for whomever and for whatever reason.

"Let us prepare," said Joseph.

It was something like praying, though the three of them remained sitting on the pale green sofa (Sarah and Joseph) and the pale green armchair (Tim) in Tim and Sarah's sitting room. In that respect, at least, it was better than going to a church where you had to kneel. But since childhood Tim had gone to church for the hymns, not the prayers, and he rather missed the singing. *Dear Lord and Father of mankind, forgive our foolish ways.* It was a shame to have a religious meeting without the hymns. This was just one of the new ways of living that Tim was having to explore, now that he was a believer.

Joseph was a tall, thin man. Taller than Tim. He had dark hair and dark skin. In the adventure books Tim had read as a child, these would have been described as saturnine looks and it would have meant he was the baddie. But Joseph had only ever done them good. Hadn't he? Joseph's hands were dry as leaves on a bonfire, his fingers long and thin. He took Tim's hand and looked directly into his eyes. It was like being seduced. Tim had always thought of seduction as being about a promise of sex between two people—a man and a woman, in his personal experience, though he had seen enough of the world (or read about it in the newspapers, at least) to know that two women might be involved, or two men. But this kind of seduction was not about sex. It promised something else. Tim held Joseph's gaze and, in spite of his misgivings, he gave in to it.

He sat on the armchair and leaned forward awkwardly to hold hands with his wife and this odd, compelling man who he didn't quite trust.

"There's someone here with us," said Joseph.

"What does he say?" asked Sarah. She was thirsty for it. She'd heard it before but she wanted more of it. She was like an addict. She was like a vampire feeding on her dead son. Tim was suddenly disgusted. He had a vision of himself standing up and running away; a dying, drug-befuddled man in hospital who has a moment of lucidity, pulls the catheters and cannulas from his body and escapes, to die free, with dignity. And then he was sorry. They were all dying. Why not die this way, slowly, leaking life, his wife beside him? They didn't have dignity or certainty. They weren't free. But at least they had each other.

"Joseph," said Tim. "What's he saying?"

"He says you're doing the right thing."

"Liam?"

"Yes, it's Liam."

Sarah broke the circle and collapsed back into the cushions of the green settee, eyes closed, hands covering her face. She looked upset, but Tim knew it gave her comfort. Liam had talked more to her in the twelve months since he had died than he had in the twelve months before that.

"Liam agrees that we should go to Torquay?"

Joseph nodded, eyes still closed. But he didn't look happy about the message.

If only there was someone other than Liam he could consult about this. Tim couldn't remember having asked Liam's opinion about even such a little thing as what film he should watch on TV on a Sunday night, or what tie he should wear to work, never mind consulting him about this scheme of Sarah's. Wasn't it bound to end disastrously?

"Can you ask him—" Tim began.

But Joseph Seppardi shook his head.

Liam was gone.

CHAPTER THREE

THE COLONEL, TRINA AND HILARY

The Seaview Motel in Torquay was to be home to the Colonel, Trina and Hilary for the next few days. It was called the Seaview Motel even though there was no view of the sea. The Colonel was known as the Colonel even though he had never seen service with the military. This was what life would be like for Trina from now on. She didn't even question it.

The Colonel and Hilary were members of an obscure religious cult, of which, until Hilary had recruited Trina, they had been the only two members.

Hilary had explained that they planned to spend the summer touring the seaside resorts of England. Trina had thought of fun fairs and hot dogs. It sounded exciting! The Colonel and Hilary had spent the winter in Croydon, not far from London. Trina had spent one night on the couch in their lodgings before they set off on the long trip from there to Torquay in a campervan. They had spent more than five hours on the road, with Trina in the back feeling sick. She was pretty sure she wouldn't have got sick if she'd traveled facing forward, eyes on the road ahead. But only the Colonel and Hilary, it seemed, were allowed to fix their eyes on the road ahead. Hilary had picked the destination, planned the route and booked the room. The Colonel was the leader of their small ensemble, though he led, like many great military men before him, from a comfortable position just behind his second in command, Hilary. Trina wasn't even third in command. She was a trainee.

"What d'you need me for, anyway?" Trina asked now, not for the first time.

"That remains to be seen," Hilary admitted. "We have to try on many coats before we find one that will fit. But you'll be a valuable part of our mission. We're offering you an opportunity. If you stick with us you might learn something that'll turn your life around." She didn't say what.

Trina had never been considered valuable by anyone before and she had learned precious little in her life so far, except how to beg and steal, and she hadn't been particularly good at either of those. They had met when Hilary knocked over a paper cup that Trina had been using to collect coins from passersby. She had been sitting on a filthy blanket in the pedestrian tunnel that led from the Royal Festival Hall in London to Waterloo. The paper cup had been on the blanket in front of her. Hilary had been hurrying past on her way to the train station. She'd knelt to pick up the scattered coins but there hadn't been that many to recover. Whatever had motivated Hilary to offer Trina something to eat and a place to stay, it wasn't admiration for the way she worked the crowds. She was keeping her reasons to herself for now. But why had Trina said yes to the offer?

It was the matter-of-factness. Hilary just seemed to assume that Trina would get up and go with her, as if the decision had already been made. There was no sympathy. She didn't seem repelled. She wasn't angry. Drunken do-gooders and post-theater commuters usually expressed one or more of those emotions at the sight of a grubby, pale girl begging in a tunnel in one of the richest cities in Europe. But most people just walked by without taking any notice.

"I was meant to find you," Hilary had said.

And Trina, tired and sick of it all, had looked at Hilary's plain, slightly earnest face, and she had agreed. She wasn't a mystical person, but Hilary had found her at the right time. She couldn't have endured that life much longer. She'd run out of choices.

So now Trina had joined the mission. She was going to learn something. Maybe after this she would be able to get a job? It was something to celebrate. There hadn't been much else to celebrate when they checked into their new temporary home in Torquay. The orange candlewick bedspreads on the twin beds in Trina and Hilary's room would have looked drab even in the 1970s when they had been purchased, though presumably they would have smelled fresher. There was a damp, unaired feel to the room. There was a little bit of mold on the seal around the bath. There was limescale on the ceramic bowl of the toilet. It was the sort of place Trina would have expected to wake up in after being plied with cheap vodka by a married pedophile. It wasn't the sort of place she'd ever imagine visiting voluntarily, unless to do harm or be harmed. If it had been booked for any other purpose, most people would want their money back. Not Hilary, of course. Because Hilary didn't care about money. She just cared about the mission.

The Colonel's room adjoined theirs. The three of them would share the bathroom at the Seaview. They'd be washing their underpants and hanging them up every evening, saving money on laundry. It was an ascetic lifestyle but it was better than living on the streets, begging for coins. What was strange for Trina was having a male presence now in her life. She didn't take much notice of the news and she never read a newspaper, but even Trina knew that absentee fathers were blamed for many things that were wrong with society, as if the lingering smell first thing in the morning in the lavatory, the razor on the bathroom shelf, the damp towel on the floor, as if any of these things could improve society. Trina didn't get it.

◆ ◆ ◆

Hilary struggled into the room like some passion play reenactment of a crucifixion, with two narrow pieces of wood about five feet long laid across her back, and a bag of nails. "We'll take first shift outside the Hotel Majestic together," she said.

Trina trembled. When you're sitting in a gloomy subway begging, you're almost invisible. Standing in front of the hotel in bright daylight would be different. The thought of it made her curl up like a photograph in a fire.

Hilary put the wood and nails on the floor. She went out to the campervan and presently came back in with two rectangles of stiff cardboard. She had a slight frame but she was wiry and strong, and Trina hadn't been brought up to say please or write thank-you letters or open doors for people, so she didn't offer to help, she just watched. Hilary put the rectangles on the floor, adjusted the angle of one of them with her toe, then took a black marker pen from her pocket and handed it over. "Make yourself a placard and you can hide behind that."

Writing wasn't one of Trina's strong points; she had barely attended school since the age of ten. She was quite artistic when it came to applying mascara and eyeliner, both of which she applied heavily enough to last a couple of days at a time. She was good with drawing. Not so good with words.

She took the cap off the pen and knelt in front of the blank rectangle. "What do I write?"

"Have you heard of Edmund Zenon?"

"No."

"He's a magician. He's here to practice blasphemy—on Easter weekend! So we need to do something about that."

"Blasphemy?" Trina twiddled the pen until the forefinger of her right hand was stained with black ink. She would be marked for twenty-four hours, like an illiterate voter in a country whose elections are rife with corruption. Blasphemy! She had no idea what it was or how to spell it. What did it matter anyway? If he was here to practice then it meant he wasn't any good at it yet, so where was the harm? But she was prepared to humor Hilary, who so far had been kind to her.

"Like what? What you gonna do?"

"There are a number of options. The Colonel would like to get him down to the beach and put his head under the waves."

The Colonel was going to drown Edmund Zenon? Whoa! Was that why Hilary had brought her here? The Colonel was going to train her to be an assassin! Trina sat open-mouthed, trying to visualize the Colonel fighting the magician with her at his side, nimble and brave. The Colonel was a big man, powerfully built. With his close-cropped white hair, his bright blue eyes and his handsome face, he resembled the Welsh actor Anthony Hopkins. But he must be nearly sixty . . . and Trina had never been in a fight before—her whole life had involved trying to avoid them or, worst case, crouching down with her head covered, taking a beating. She'd never used her fists, let alone a sword or whatever you needed to defeat someone who was magic. So unless Edmund Zenon was really puny, how could they win? And even if he was puny, couldn't he use magic to defeat them? Trina imagined Edmund dressed in a wizard's robes, zapping the Colonel with a wand as the Colonel tried to drown him.

"Trina!"

"What?"

"We want to save his soul."

"Oh." Trina couldn't hide her disappointment. "So why not do that, then? Instead of the placard?"

"Because I'm not sure if Edmund Zenon has a soul that can be saved."

Poor Edmund Zenon. Trina wrote a piece of advice on her placard that she would follow herself, if she could: GO HOME! The magician might not have a soul but Trina was willing to bet he had a home to go to. She'd have traded one for the other if she knew how to do it.

CHAPTER FOUR
MADAME NOVA

Madame Nova earned a little money telling fortunes for tourists in Torquay. She used tarot cards, but would read palms at a push, if that's what the punters wanted. She also had a costume shop, A Little of What You Fancy, the name taken from a bawdy song Marie Lloyd used to sing in the musical hall at Hackney in East London back in the late nineteenth century.

She loved her dressing-up shop: wigs, moustaches, face paints, wings, silvery knitted chainmail armor, helmets, false ears, false teeth, false legs . . . Well, of course everything in it was false, mocked up to look more elaborate and expensive than it was, created to serve some individual's fantasy for one evening. Madame Nova catered mostly for the boozy prenuptial celebrations of hen nights and stag nights, and Halloween of course. The shop was overstocked but still she couldn't resist the occasional foray up to town—to London—to buy unwanted items from the National Theatre or the Royal Opera House that she saw advertised in *The Stage*, the weekly newspaper for actors and craftspeople involved in the profession. The wigs! Each one was a work of art and, quite frankly, wasted on the silly girls in Torquay who wanted to wear them to go drinking and pick up fishermen in town, ending the night puking their cut-price cocktails into the gutter with their boobs hanging over their ankles. If asked by one of these vulgar creatures, Madame Nova usually put the price for one of her wigs at a hundred pounds for one night's hire: something silly to deter casual use. It wasn't good business sense but it made sense to Madame Nova. Not much else did.

She remembered some famous trickster—was it Harry Houdini?—who had wanted to be buried with a telephone in case he woke up, realized he hadn't died, and needed to communicate with friends above ground to tell them to come and dig him out. Madame Nova had a phone in the flat where she lived above the shop. But she rarely made calls on it and it rarely rang, except with the occasional automated message telling her she could be entitled to compensation for a car accident—she didn't drive—or that she had won the lottery in Liechtenstein and she should call back with her bank account details to claim her winnings. It hadn't provided her with any useful communication since she had moved to Torquay, so if she needed to persuade anyone that she was alive after she had died, she would probably choose some instrument other than the telephone to be buried with.

Madame Nova had been living here in the shadowlands—or, to give it its proper name, Torquay—for more years than she would wish to remember, retired from the bright lights and cultural excitements of London, away from old friends and old lovers, away from the acting profession—though the training came in useful, of course, with the fortune-telling. She was good at interpreting nonvisual cues. She had a memory for tricky little bits of information murmured during the course of casual conversation, and, most important of all, she could deliver a line as though the listener's life depended on it. And perhaps, this weekend, someone's life might depend on taking note of what she had to say. Because Madame Nova was about to depart from her usual script, and what she had to say was significant.

A mob of silly girls came into the shop, their business as obvious as if they had carried in front of them a big banner proclaiming HEN NIGHT! They spent some time choosing wings and tiaras and a cheap wedding veil made out of old net curtain for the bride. They tested the light-up wands and waved them around, imagining chasing fit young men up the High Street with them, and then being chased back down again for a kiss. Then one of them asked if Madame Nova would read the palm of the bride-to-be.

Madame Nova, with her big, baggy careworn eyes and her mouth looking as if it would chew itself off if anyone tried to chase her down the High Street and give her a kiss, took the girl's hand solemnly and said she would give her a reading for free.

"Your marriage will be blessed with two healthy boys," she said.

"Two more or two in total?" asked Jackie Churchill, the bride-to-be.

"I see two boys in your hand."

"Phew! That's a relief! Two's enough, I reckon."

"Your Tyrone's about to start nursery, isn't he?" said the girl next to Jackie. It was Mandy Miller, one of the receptionists up at the Hotel Majestic.

"Already started, Mandy. So, OK, they're not babies. But she's bang on with the number." Jackie blushed with pride. "And I do feel blessed with my boys."

Madame Nova inclined her head, to show that she was not surprised that she had been proved right. She had no intention of saying that she had passed by McDonald's a few times and seen Jackie inside with her sons, and that was where she'd got her information, not in the creases of Jackie's palm. Now, where was she likely to go on honeymoon? Was the boyfriend employed? She thought he was.

"You've a nice holiday coming up somewhere . . . Thailand? The Maldives?"

"Ooh!" said the bridesmaids-to-be. "Clever!"

Jackie nodded, impressed. "We're booked to go to the Maldives."

Two of the younger women giggled and nudged each other. "Anyone going to meet their husband at Jackie's wedding?"

A girl at the back of the group called out, "How about the hen night tomorrow? Any luck for any of us finding a fella?" She was making the battery run down on a lighted wand by turning it on and waving it, and turning it off again; turning it on and waving it, turning it off again. Dawn Miller, Mandy's sister. Dawn was as daft as Mandy was sensible. Never mind. Madame Nova wasn't going to get upset about a battery in a cheap wand. They'd already paid for the hire of it.

She turned her eyes on the group, the future bride's hand still in hers. Madame Nova had played Ophelia but she had never played Lady Macbeth, though she'd have been good in the role. The tragic witterings of the cast-off Danish would-be bride had always irritated her, and she called on her contempt for Ophelia now to deliver her next line. Any passing casting director would surely have admired the performance and whisked her off to London to star as Lady M in "the Scottish Play." But there never were any casting directors passing Madame Nova's shop, which was one of the many reasons why she had moved here. Still, she gave it her all.

"You girls had better be careful this weekend." She frowned as she examined Jackie's palm.

"What you on about?" Jackie tried to pull her hand away.

"No. I had better not say any more. It will just worry you."

"Not the kids? Not Dave?" That was all Jackie needed—something bad happening less than a month before her wedding day! She wasn't even sure she wanted to get married. She'd said yes when Dave had proposed. But she'd been drunk at the time and so had he. They'd each been expecting the other to wriggle out of it but here they were, the registry office booked for next weekend, a wedding gift list chosen at Debenhams, and a reception with disco and cash bar at the Hotel Majestic for family, work colleagues and friends.

A laugh and a joke was one thing. Having her fortune told was a bit of fun. She'd taken it with a pinch of salt. They *were* going to the Maldives for their honeymoon, as it happened. But didn't everyone? Bad news was different. You had to respect bad news. You had to fear it, to make sure it didn't happen. She looked at Madame Nova with as much fear and respect as if the fortune-teller had knocked on her front door wearing a police uniform.

"No," said Madame Nova. "Not your family. Not you, either. You'll be fine."

"What, then?"

Dawn Miller called from the back. "C'mon. Let's get out of here."

"Shut up, Dawn," said Jackie. "I want to hear what she has to say."

"You're familiar with Oscar Wilde?" Madame Nova asked Dawn. *"A dreamer is one who can only find his way by moonlight—"*

"You what?"

"A dreamer is one who can only find his way by moonlight, and his punishment is that he sees Dawn before the rest of the world." She had misquoted, slightly.

"Very funny," said Dawn sourly.

"We're not interested in Oscar Wilde," said Jackie Churchill.

Madame Nova looked once more at Jackie's palm, then she looked solemnly round at the group. "We all like to drown our sorrows at the weekend, don't we?"

It seemed like a trick question. What was wrong with having a drink? Nobody said anything.

"The gods are no different. This weekend they will drown one of their sorrows . . . and it seems they propose doing it in Torquay."

"Eh?" said Jackie. She turned to her friends. "What's she on about?"

"Have any of you girls caused the gods to be sorrowful? If not, you'll be safe."

"It's the good ones that get taken young. That's what my gran used to say," Dawn protested.

"I've looked at Jackie's hand and it's as plain as the pimple on your face, Dawn. Someone will die this weekend."

"Well, that's a right downer." Jackie pulled her hand away at last.

Mandy Miller put her arm round Jackie and began to lead her out of the shop. "Only one way to fix that. The pub! Come *on*. It's a four-day weekend."

"The pub!" Dawn and the others called as they followed Jackie and Mandy.

Before they had reached the Lamb and Dragon pub on the High Street, the girls had managed to make a joke of it, with some of the feistier ones repeating their favorite line: "Have any of you girls caused the gods to be sorrowful?"

"If anyone gets drowned this weekend, it should be her," said Dawn, touching her chin with her fingertips, checking to see whether she really did have a pimple. "She's the most nastiest person in Torquay."

Madame Nova had enjoyed giving them a little scare. She had got caught up in the wordplay that involved drowning sorrows, unfortunately. She was better at delivering the lines than she was at inventing them. She had never enjoyed improv. Never mind, she'd had a little fun. Fun came by even less often than casting directors since she had moved to Torquay.

Madame Nova gave a bitter little smile, locked the door of her shop, and went out the back to look at her collection of wigs. She could never choose between her three favorites, which had been crafted for a pantomime. They were two foot tall and brightly colored, each of them with a false panel of hair at the front which could be opened to reveal, in the yellow one, a cuckoo clock, with a bird that flew out and back in again on a wire and made a chirping noise; in the pink one, a tiny gun that could be operated with a lever and fired with quite a loud bang; and in the red wig, two fingers on a waxwork hand that moved up and down to make a vulgar Anglo-Saxon gesture.

But today Madame Nova got no pleasure from the thought of putting one of them on. *Someone will die this weekend,* she had said. Was it really going to happen?

She went upstairs and opened a bottle of Merlot to drown her sorrows.

CHAPTER FIVE
ON THE TRAIN

It was Friday morning, about ten o'clock. Emily Castles stood next to Dr. Muriel on the concourse at Paddington train station in London, her little suitcase by her side, looking up at the changing configuration of orange lights on the electronic departures board. Her neck ached. As soon as the allocated platform for their train was announced, it would be the cue for waiting travelers to rush toward the platform with the fierce competitiveness of shoppers in the January sales, even though most of them would have a seat reservation. And then there it was: platform nine. They were off! Dr. Muriel jabbed an elbow at Emily to make sure she was paying attention, picked up the long metal handle of her suitcase, tapped her silver-topped cane on the ground in front of her, then she charged toward the platform, pulling her case behind like a horse trailer, Emily trotting beside her. They hurled themselves onto the train, slightly breathless, and then settled into two window seats either side of a small table—a premium position. Despite the rush to claim it, they had the table to themselves for the whole journey. The train wasn't crowded after all. It was March, out of season for Torquay.

Emily sat back in her seat and looked out of the window. The train was still in the station. The doors were open and passengers were boarding. But when the train in the next platform slowly began to move off, Emily experienced a strange trick of the mind as her eyes told her head that *her* train must be moving. A look down at the platform readjusted the signal from Emily's eyes to her brain, reassuring her that the train she was sitting in was motionless.

Across from her, Dr. Muriel was anything but motionless. She exhibited all the signs of busy enjoyment that made her such a likeable companion. She put her handbag and a newspaper on the table in front of her and shrugged out of her emerald-green corduroy jacket, standing up and sitting down at least twice to do it, and then standing up again and going onto tiptoes to tuck her jacket onto the storage rail above her head. Then she insisted on storing Emily's jacket for her, so that Emily had to stand up and shrug out of it, and hand it over, and sit down, and Dr. Muriel had to go up on tiptoes again, scrunching up Emily's jacket and stuffing it into the very small space available. Next, she grasped the handles of her handbag, which was enormous and heavy looking, and eyed up the luggage rack above the head of a nervous-looking young man sitting across the aisle from them at another window seat.

"No!" he said. He stood up, alarmed. Then he lowered his voice, a little embarrassed. "Do you want me to help you with that?"

"Thank you, no." Dr. Muriel put her handbag on the table and shoved it over toward the window where it was more or less out of the way. She looked pleased as she sat down. "We're a regular pair of jack-in-the-boxes." Emily suspected that her friend found ordinary things entertaining because she spent so little time doing ordinary things—usually she was preoccupied with philosophical conundrums.

The lad across from them sat down again, too. He was in his twenties, about Emily's age, pale and fragile looking, with the intense, hungry expression common to vampires and postgraduate students. He was wearing a khaki knitted hat that looked like a tea cozy. It was probably considered fashionable in the circles he moved in. Behind him, as the train moved off quietly and on time, the world outside the window slid back like a panel of scenery in a play.

"It's strange, isn't it?" Dr. Muriel said to Emily.

Lots of things seemed strange to Dr. Muriel because she had an off-kilter way of looking at things. Emily stayed quiet and waited for an explanation.

"I should be impressed by the silence that accompanies a modern train's departure from the station. But I'm not. Now, why is that?"

"It feels like the train's trying to sneak out of the station and leave some of the passengers behind?"

"Aha! Very good."

"It would explain why everyone runs to the platform in such a rush."

"Of course, I don't really believe that a *train* is capable of being sneaky." Dr. Muriel was suddenly sharp, as if Emily had been trying to catch her out. "But I must say, I miss the trains from my childhood with their slamming doors and whistle-blowing guards. Does that make me sound ancient?"

"I remember slamming doors and whistle-blowing guards."

"What do you think of the idea that a train is no longer *just a train* when it starts to move—that when so many souls are riding alongside each other, all of us trusting this beast with our lives, we are transformed and combined into one entity? We submit to a mutually altered consciousness. We're children clinging to a serpent's back as it wiggles and whooshes through the English countryside."

"Are you planning on saying something like that at the conference?"

"No indeed! Much too fanciful. But I thought it might appeal to you." Dr. Muriel was very cheerful. But then she was always cheerful. She clasped her hands together and sat back and smiled, looking out of the window. "I find it very interesting the way you feel the presence of Jessie quite strongly, even though it's a while now since she died. The belief in angels has always held fairly steady. But there does seem to be a resurgence of interest in spiritualism. Dead relatives. Dead pets. Spirit guides."

"I don't see her *ghost*. I don't talk to her spirit."

"One doesn't judge, of course. One simply asks why."

"I just sometimes think, you know, wouldn't it be nice if Jessie was here? Jessie as she was in her prime. Not the old lady who lay all day sleeping by the kitchen door."

"So there's a time travel element?"

"No!"

Dr. Muriel smiled and looked out of the window. She was facing forwards, Emily was facing backwards—only able to appreciate the English countryside after they had left it behind them, as if she was hopelessly nostalgic.

As they sped away from London toward Torquay, Emily saw blurry trees. She saw swings and plastic climbing frames in primary colors in the long, narrow gardens of terraced houses sloping down toward the embankments at the sides of the railway tracks. She saw the purple spikes of buddleia growing unchecked along the embankments, and leaf-strewn pathways leading up to grassy hills. She thought how much Jessie would have enjoyed running through the piles of leaves, picking up sticks that were impracticably big and trying to run with them in her mouth. Then she thought about the strange assignment she'd been hired for, because of her "sensitivity."

"Do you think Gerald believes Edmund Zenon's going to die this weekend?"

"Ah! Interesting question. I don't know. But I *do* know he's ambitious. He's overspent on this conference and he wants to use Lady Lacey Carmichael's legacy to help him publicize it so he can fund the next one."

"What about Peg?"

"You know she gives fashion advice in the newspapers based on conversations she claims to have with Princess Diana in heaven? I like her, from the little I know of her. She'd be tremendous fun at a dinner party. But I do think she ought to be called Preposterous Peg."

"Could she have invented these messages about a man drowning in Torquay so she can publicize her book somehow?"

"I had the impression that she was sincere, didn't you? But even if she *believes* that she has received a message from the spirit world about a death by drowning, does that mean she has? Based on the data available from the study of similar cases over the years, it's highly improbable."

"Maybe she's had information from a real live person? I mean, a phone call or something."

"Ah! Interesting. That may be so."

"I think I need to treat this investigation as if someone really might be murdered. I've accepted the job so I want to do it properly. I'm going to see if I can identify any suspects, establish possible motives."

"Where will you start?"

"I'll start with you." Emily opened her notebook and got out her pen. "You've been to these sorts of conferences before, haven't you? And nothing like this has ever happened."

"The weirdest thing was when Miriam Starling got the heel of her shoe caught in a grating as she crossed the road. She was pulled to safety by two German professors as a bus came round the corner. The bus ran over her shoe and she had to hop back to the hotel."

"So . . . not very weird at all then?"

"Heh! Well, it was dramatic and quite amusing once we knew she was safe. I'm afraid we laughed a lot at the hopping—Miriam laughed more than anyone, she's a very good sport. But it couldn't be classed as a supernatural event. No one had predicted that it might happen."

"So these conferences have been going on for years with nothing extraordinary happening. Now Peg, and dozens of other psychics up and down the country, are having visions about a man drowning. Why?"

"Why indeed?" said Dr. Muriel. She preferred asking questions to answering them.

"It seems the big difference between this conference and the others is that Edmund Zenon is coming to Torquay and he's offering lots of money."

There was the sound of a little gasp and then a long, soft sigh from one end of the carriage as the automatic door slid open quickly and then closed again slowly. The conductor's voice called, "Tickets, please!"

Dr. Muriel rustled in her handbag and found a bag of treacle toffees before she found the train tickets Gerald Ayode had bought for her and Emily to travel to Torquay.

She offered the toffees to Emily and unwrapped one for herself. "You need to make time to enjoy yourself. Treat your stay in Torquay like a holiday. The Hotel Majestic is a lovely, big, white Art Deco building on a cliff above the bay, facing down toward the sea. It has plenty of amenities, including indoor and outdoor pools, two restaurants, a bar, a ballroom, a spa, a gymnasium, conference rooms, a business center and free Wi-Fi. There are thick white towels in the bathrooms, crisp white sheets in the bedrooms, duvets for winter, complimentary slippers, complimentary bathrobes, complimentary fancy hand creams, shampoos and soaps. If you believed in ghosts, then the Hotel Majestic would be the perfect location to watch for guests from a more glamorous era, when Torquay's golden beachfront was an alternative to the French Riviera, and the French Riviera was as glamorous as anywhere could possibly be. I know you've been miserable stuck in that office for the last two weeks, Emily. When Gerald came to me asking for advice about how to get the report done, I thought of you immediately."

People like Dr. Muriel were always trying to get Emily to do something else for a living, as if she worked in offices on temporary assignments because it had never occurred to her to do anything more interesting with her time, like apply to NASA to be an astronaut. They meant well but they didn't seem to realize she did this kind of work because it suited her. She might moan about it sometimes but at least she could pay the bills. Yes, it would be lovely to be a movie star or an astronaut. Or even a "future crimes investigator." But Emily had never met anyone who earned their living that way.

"What's funny?" asked Dr. Muriel.

"I was thinking about trying to earn a living as a future crimes investigator."

"Too bad you didn't have time to get some business cards printed." Dr. Muriel twinkled mischievously. "You could have put a picture of Jessie on the front."

"It's a shame you have to work while you're there."

"The work's almost the best thing about it, apart from the morning swim. There'll be friends I haven't seen in a year—it's fascinating to see how they've changed and grown older; rather like time-lapse photography. Old friends, new ideas, fish and chips on the sea front, and Edmund Zenon's challenge, which will annoy just about everyone, which will add to the fun. If someone wins—which I very much doubt, but you never know—it will be like Christmas Day and New Year's Eve and my birthday, all in one."

"Do you know if he's putting up his own money for the challenge?"

"He is!" The young man in the knitted hat leaned across the

aisle to join the conversation. "Fifty thousand pounds of his own money, and it's, like, in a certified account, ready and waiting."

The conductor had worked his way down the train carriage and now stood by their table. "Tickets, please!"

Dr. Muriel showed him the tickets and offered him a toffee, which he declined with the professionalism of a policeman who has been offered a drink on duty.

"Are you going to make a bid for the money?" Emily asked the lad with the knitted hat.

"Nuh. I do magic tricks."

"I love magic! What kind?"

"Close-up magic. Card tricks." He made a swan's-neck movement with his right hand and produced a deck of cards from his sleeve, fanning the cards and holding out the queen of hearts for Emily to see. He grinned. "Once they know Edmund Zenon's in town, everyone's gonna be milling about, hoping to see something. If he's busy, maybe they'll pay to see me."

"How did you know he'd be down here?" said Dr. Muriel. "He's attending an academic conference."

"His picture was on the Royal Festival Hall. It's on Twitter. People have been talking about it."

"And you saw it and you thought . . . what?" Emily got out her notebook and pen.

"I thought, I can do twenty, maybe thirty tricks an hour, working the crowd in the street. My girlfriend said we should come down, try and make some money."

"I think it's time your girlfriend made her appearance, don't you?" said the conductor. "Passengers have to pay for their tickets, whether they're taking up a seat or not. You're a magician, are you? Why don't you use your magic wand and make her appear?"

Emily stared at the empty forward-facing seat across the aisle.

Sure enough, little by little, the girlfriend materialized, from the feet up. Dr. Muriel and Emily exchanged a quick look with each other, impressed. Then they turned back to watch the impromptu show. The first part of her they saw was a foot in a pink sock inside a pink spotted sneaker. Then the other foot, in matching sock and sneaker. Then her legs in a pair of jeans, followed by the rest of her. She looked as though she had hardly any flesh on her bones under the layers of warm woolly clothes she was wearing, which included a baggy sweater and a long stripy scarf wound several times around her neck. Finally, her face: she had fairish hair cut in a long bob that fell to her jawbone, and very little makeup. She had not been invisible so much as hidden. And strictly speaking, she didn't materialize so much as slowly reveal herself by dangling first one leg, then another, from the luggage rack above her boyfriend's head where she had been concealed, folded up behind the coat that had been laid along it.

She lowered herself to the floor beneath, light as a cat and almost as languorous, and took her seat by the window. She made a great show of stretching her arms and yawning, as if she'd been so tired she couldn't help but lie down and go to sleep up there, even before the train had left Paddington. She was a better contortionist than she was an actress. As the conductor waited, she put her hand in the back pocket of her jeans and produced a ticket.

The conductor looked at it and handed it back. "That's a super-saver. Forty pounds to upgrade to a full-price ticket or you'll have to get off at the next stop."

"Look," said the lad with the knitted hat to the conductor, "I'm sorry."

"Sorry, mate." In this kind of transaction, you had to have one person who was sorry and another who was prepared to forgive. You couldn't have two people who were sorry. If the conductor was sorry, too, then Emily knew there was no hope that this girl would be allowed to continue her journey without paying full fare. "You've got to have the correct ticket to travel on the train. This is the only nonstop service to Torquay this morning and you can't use the cheap tickets on it. Come on now. Let's have a look at yours."

The boyfriend's ticket was fine. The conductor clipped it and turned back to deal with the girl.

"I'm sorry," she said. Well that was no good! You couldn't have three people who were sorry, even if none of them sounded sorry at all. "I don't have forty pounds."

"I'm sorry!" Dr. Muriel interrupted. Now it was getting out of hand. "I don't mean to intrude, but I wonder if I might pay for this young woman's ticket. My fare's paid for. In fact all my expenses are paid because I'm giving a talk at the conference. I'm jolly lucky because it's one of the things I look forward to most in the year. I'd happily buy a ticket if I had to, but it's all free."

"Well . . ." said the conductor.

"I insist," said Dr. Muriel, addressing the young woman directly. "Since I don't have to buy my ticket, I would like to buy yours." As the conductor handed over her credit card receipt, Dr. Muriel said to him, "How did you know that young woman was tucked away in the luggage rack? Emily didn't even know—did you, Emily?—and she's a brilliant sleuth."

The stowaway and her boyfriend looked at Emily as if Dr. Muriel had said she was a talking donkey.

The conductor tapped the side of his nose, indicating that the secret must remain his and he would never reveal it. Nobody pleaded with him to change his mind so he revealed it anyway. "Took a walk down the outside of the train before boarding was announced, saw these two hop on. Usually if there's any funny business with the tickets, they get on early and hide in the toilets. I had a look to see what they were up to and saw the young lady getting up there.

Eyes and intuition." He made a fork of the first two fingers of his right hand and pointed at his eyes, to help his audience imagine the process. "Nothing fancy compared to the methods of Miss Sherlock Holmes here, I expect."

"That's the best kind of investigating," said Emily modestly. "Using your eyes and observing what you see."

"Ah yes!" said Dr. Muriel. "How many of us really look? How many of us really *see* when we look?"

As the conductor made his way back down the carriage away from them, Emily heard once again the sound of the little gasp and then the long, soft sigh as the automatic door slid open quickly and then closed again slowly, the drama over for now.

Emily sat back and she, too, sighed a long, soft sigh as the stress of the last two weeks' work escaped from her. She was on holiday. Sort of . . . She looked out of the window at the canal boats on the river that now wound its way alongside the train as it headed southwest past Reading. She saw sheep and cornfields. She saw ferns, fir trees, horses, houses, ducks, geese. She saw swans. When you spent all your time in a big city, it was easy to forget that people were living here in the countryside in a storybook world, a world of canal locks and cart horses. An unLondon. Emily saw alpacas, or some sort of long-necked, furry animal not native to England, trotting purposefully through a field.

The young couple interrupted her thoughts by introducing themselves as Alice and Ben. "We'll pay you back, soon as we make some money, Muriel," said Alice. "We'll be down by the Lamb and Dragon pub or maybe by the beach. Shall I give you my number so you can give us a ring before you come down?"

"It doesn't matter. Don't worry about it."

"I'll write it in your notebook, Emma."

"Emily."

"Emily." Alice put out her hands for Emily's notebook and pen. The train went into a tunnel and they were briefly cut off from daytime and sunlight. Across the aisle from Emily there was now a second Alice, reflected in the window next to her and then in the window on the opposite side of the train, and then projected beyond the window beside her so she seemed to hover in the blackness outside the train, at the same distance from the window as the original Alice inside it, the ghost of a living girl, keeping pace with them all, writing down a number that Dr. Muriel would never call.

Inside the train, at the table behind Emily and Dr. Muriel, a man now began to make himself a sandwich, assembling the ingredients from a Tupperware container. He had brought a knife to spread the butter on a soft white roll, some ham. The process was comfortingly old-fashioned. Outside, as the train emerged into the daylight again, Emily saw two piebald ponies, nose to nose, keeping each other company. She saw a heron in a muddy puddle in a field. And because she was facing backwards as she traveled, because she was looking out at events that had happened a microsecond before the light hit the retina in the back of her eye and her brain made sense of it, there was nothing she could do to change any of it. She felt soothed. Relieved.

Dr. Muriel noticed and approved. "The sea air will blow all your troubles away," she said.

But trouble was blowing into Torquay. And Emily and Dr. Muriel were about to get caught up in the middle of it.

CHAPTER SIX
THE HOTEL MAJESTIC

As the train arrived at Torquay station just before one o'clock, Emily got her first glimpse of the town. She looked out across the sweep of the bay to where hotels and houses looked down onto the sea from a clifftop. There was something jauntily continental about the rows of yachts and pleasure cruisers in the harbor, which lay surrounded by shops and restaurants at the bottom of the hill.

As she left the train, she saw a sputnik-shaped booth plastered with posters advertising tourist excursions by boat, bus and train. There were day trips to Paignton and Brixham and Agatha Christie's house. There were fishing trips, and rides around the pier for people who enjoyed being towed on a large inflatable banana. And there was a poster showing Edmund Zenon in his walking-on-water pose. This one had white lettering handwritten over the top of it: MEET ME IN THE SMELL OF A BOOK BOOKSHOP, TORQUAY, 4 PM FRIDAY. Emily took out her notebook and wrote down the time.

Outside the station there was an advertising billboard with news of upcoming shows at the local theater—mostly tribute acts to long-dead pop stars. They might have been ghosts secretly congregating in Torquay to be close at hand for Edmund Zenon's paranormal challenge, while masquerading as tribute acts. But Emily thought it unlikely. Tacked onto the billboard there were two large, glossy posters advertising the challenge. Here was Edmund again in top hat and cape, walking on water. But these had been defaced. Someone had scrawled *Go Home!* on top of them. Emily wrote that in her notebook, too.

Emily stopped to read the sign put up by the tourist board just outside Torquay train station:

WELCOME TO THE ENGLISH RIVIERA, TORQUAY.
TWINNED WITH HAMELIN AND HELLEVOETSLUIS.

"*Hell-vote-sluice* sounds like a device to separate the souls from the bodies of dead people in a mortuary, and flush the unwanted bits away," she said to Dr. Muriel.

"What an imagination you have! It's a city in Belgium. I believe they say *hell-vouts-laus*. Much less alarming, don't you think? More like a coleslaw than a disposal system for mortal remains. Come on!"

Dr. Muriel unhooked her silver-topped walking stick from her pull-along case and gestured toward the Hotel Majestic, only a few yards from the train station, looking out onto a gray sea under an overcast sky from on top of a hill.

"It gladdens my heart as soon as I step off the train and see it. Fresh air! Sea views! What do you think?"

"I think we might have trouble getting past that lot."

Up ahead, a small crowd had gathered outside the main entrance, which was at the back of the hotel, facing the train station and away from the sea. Emily looked to see whether there was another doorway round the side that they could use. But Dr. Muriel moved forward fearlessly, waving her cane as if she was scattering pigeons in a park.

Most of the people in the crowd were standing around, hands in pockets, looking cold. A feral-looking teenage girl in a hooded top was holding a placard with GO HOME! written on it. The girl slunk back as Dr. Muriel approached, pressing her sleeve under her nose as if she could smell something rotten. Most of the bottom half of her face was covered but Emily saw pale skin, dark brown eyes, dark brown hair. Next to the girl was a wiry woman in her forties with another placard. This one said SAVE YOUR SOUL and, underneath that, PLEDGE AND PLUNGE. The woman had short, light brown hair and she was wearing very little make-up. She was dressed in jeans, a thick knitted sweater and a black workman's jacket. Her eyes were a muddy green; soft and speckled like a feather from a garden bird. There was a challenge in her expression. Emily went over to talk to her. The true start of her investigation!

"Hello. I'm Emily. Are you here to protest against Edmund Zenon?"

The woman rotated the placard a quarter of an inch. "I'm Hilary. This is Trina." Trina didn't make eye contact. "We're here to save his soul, if we can. Come down to the beach later, if you'd like to learn more about it. About five o'clock?"

There was an excited murmur from the small crowd. A man called out, "Someone's coming!"

Emily and Dr. Muriel turned and watched as a man in his mid-thirties in a shiny blue suit made his way toward the hotel entrance. He had thinning sandy hair and lightly plucked eyebrows. Three brown, long-haired miniature dachshunds on blue leads walked in front of him. The dogs were wearing blue coats that matched their owner's suit.

"Is it him?" a woman called from the crowd. "Is it the magician?"

But the man in the blue suit wasn't the man they were waiting for. The people in the crowd shifted about, raising their eyebrows at each other and stamping their feet to make the point that they'd put themselves to *a lot* of trouble by standing out here in the cold to wait for Edmund Zenon.

"Come on," said Dr. Muriel to Emily. "We'd better go in. It'll get crazy when Edmund arrives."

"It's crazy now," said Emily.

"Gerald would insist on making the conference bigger this year. Bigger is not always better. But there's no point saying that to a man."

Two security guards stood together at the door, making a two-man wall of muscle to prevent the crowd from coming in. They stood aside to let Dr. Muriel and Emily pass after inspecting a print-out of an email confirming their hotel booking for the weekend.

Senior receptionist Mandy Miller, wearing a badge with her name and job title on it, greeted Emily and Dr. Muriel with a pleasant smile as they checked in. Noticing Dr. Muriel's cane, she nodded over to where two wheelchairs were folded up by the entrance, beneath a plaque proclaiming that the Hotel Majestic was a winner of the Wheely Good Hotel award, given to hotels in the Devon and Dorset areas after a vote among guests with mobility problems. "Will you be wanting a wheelchair during your stay, madam? We keep those here for use by guests."

"Doctor."

"You need a doctor?"

"My name's Doctor Muriel Crowther. I shan't be needing a wheelchair, thank you."

The man in the blue suit with the dachshunds was now behind Emily, waiting his turn while Mandy brought up the details of Dr. Muriel's room reservation on the computer.

Outside, there was a commotion. Emily could hear clapping, cheering and whistling.

"Don't let anyone in unless they've got a reservation, Derek," Mandy said to the bigger of the two security guards. He remained silent, his back toward Mandy, betraying neither gratitude nor resentment for this advice about how to do his job.

Then the gap between the two men bulged open and Edmund Zenon emerged, smiling and triumphant, like a participant in a pageant that evokes the birth of a hero, with the security guards playing the part of the birth canal. Edmund was tall and slim, wearing an elegant gray sweater and a good pair of jeans. He went straight up to the reception desk at the hotel, nodding pleasantly to Dr. Muriel and Emily as he edged in next to them. He smelled of fresh rain on cut grass. His teeth were perfect. He was amazing.

"Hello there . . . Mandy"—he discreetly checked her name badge—"I'm Edmund Zenon. Is my room ready?"

Mandy looked as though she was trying to memorize every moment of their brief exchange. She handed over the key to Edmund's room. "Number thirty-six. Lovely view of the sea. The elevator's over there to the right in the lobby."

"Number thirty-six?" said Dr. Muriel, frowning.

"Do you need help with your bags?" Mandy asked Edmund.

"No thanks. My technical guy's already checked in. He's got most of the luggage." He took the key, smiled, and stalked off toward the elevator.

"I wonder if I could have a word?" Emily said, taking a few steps after him. "It's quite important."

"Sure!" The doors to the elevator opened. Edmund stepped in. "Call me," he said as the doors closed. The elevator ascended.

OK. So that hadn't gone as well as it might have. Emily went back to Reception, where Mandy was handing over a key to Dr. Muriel.

"And for you we have a lovely room in the eaves at the top of the hotel."

"Does it face the sea?"

"I'm afraid not, no."

"I think number thirty-six is the room I usually stay in. Is there a balcony overlooking the sea? French windows?"

"Oh. I don't know what happened! I was going to give that key to you. Maybe he hypnotized me?"

"Can't you call his room and tell him there's been a mistake?" Emily suggested.

"I can't, no. Hotel policy, I'm sorry. I'm not allowed to change the room now that it's been allocated to Mr. Zenon." Mandy completed the check-in arrangements—Emily had also been allocated a lovely inward-facing room in the eaves—and handed over their keys.

"What did Edmund say?" Dr. Muriel asked as she walked with Emily to the elevator. "Did you talk to him about Peg and her prophecy?"

"He didn't say anything, he just fobbed me off by telling me to call him. Obviously I don't have his number. I'll have to try again, next time I see him. I think I need to sit down with him and make a list of his enemies."

"Well," said Dr. Muriel to Emily, "if it's any use to you, you can put my name on the list."

"Muriel!"

"Oh, look out. It's Miriam Starling."

"The one who lost her shoe at the last conference and had to hop?" Emily saw an elegant woman in a sleek black dress, waving at them from her seat in the lobby next to two other chic-looking women. She was embarrassed to realize she'd assumed that all academics must wear shabby tweed and crushed corduroy.

Dr. Muriel put her right hand on her cane for balance and hopped on her left foot, like a participant in a Legs, Bums and Tums class. "Hop, Emily! Hop! Miriam will find it amusing."

Emily hopped. She was someone who was happy to go along with other people's suggestions, so long as she didn't feel they were taking advantage. And anyway, who doesn't want to do something that might make another person laugh?

Miriam and the women who were with her stood and hopped, too. They didn't just laugh, they guffawed. It was infectious. Soon Emily was laughing, too.

"The women with her are the German professors," said Dr. Muriel. "I won't go and say hello. If you stop and talk to one group, you end up talking to everybody, and I have never seen the place so busy."

Men and women were sitting, standing, stooping, crouching and leaning in every available space in the hotel, between leather sofas, armchairs, reproduction antiques and a grand piano. There was the low, buzzy noise of dozens of indistinguishable conversations.

"I suppose that's what Twitter would sound like if you could hear it," said Emily.

"Oh! But it's like the anticipatory chatter before a concert in a large auditorium—such a happy sound. Now you make me want to try it."

"Twitter? Well, don't tell Gerald. He'll want you to broadcast your thoughts about the conference."

"I don't mind doing that at all. But I shall broadcast telepathically, for the benefit of the psychics who are joining us for the first time." Dr. Muriel kept silent and stared solemnly at Emily, as if testing her method.

Emily put her fingertips lightly to her temples, playing along. "You're thinking . . . we should dump our suitcases and then get some lunch."

"Marvelous! Peg was right, you do have the gift. It just needs a little development. I'll meet you in the restaurant in ten minutes. If you get there before me, I'll have a double helping of hashtags with sweet chili sauce." Dr. Muriel disappeared into the crowd. But Emily could still hear her laughing.

◆ ◆ ◆

After she had checked into her room, Emily went back downstairs to look around. The blue-suited man had managed to find himself a space to sit with his dogs in an area between the lobby and the hotel's Riviera Lounge. Emily squeezed past a flushed woman with badly cut gray-blonde hair to reach him. She bent to pet the dogs.

"Elvis, Shirley and Eddie," their owner told her. "I'm a psychic. Bobby Blue Suit, they call me."

"I'm Emily. Your dogs are very sweet. Are they . . . do they help you in your work?"

Bobby tapped the end of his nose, signaling the need for discretion. "Can't say too much. Got to keep the tricks of the trade pretty close. You got a dog, Emily? No! Don't tell me . . ." He closed his eyes and breathed in deeply. Then he opened his eyes again. "I'm going to say yes."

"Well, there is a dog. Jessie. But she's not here. She's not alive."

"A spirit guide?" Bobby Blue Suit suddenly looked much less friendly, as if he suspected Emily might be a rival for the fifty thousand pounds. "What breed, if you don't mind my asking?"

"Golden retriever."

"Clever choice! Course, I favor the daxies myself. Very inquisitive breed of dog."

"Look, I'm not challenging for the fifty thousand pounds. I'm here . . . I'm kind of a paranormal investigator."

"Oh." Bobby relaxed. "Here to see fair play? That's a good idea. I wondered how they were going to manage things for the challenge tomorrow. They haven't said much about it, have they? Just, meet in the Green Room at ten o'clock and, when you come out of the Ballroom, whether you win or lose, don't say anything to anybody. Did you have to sign a confidentiality agreement like the rest of us?"

"I'm not connected to Edmund Zenon."

Bobby closed his eyes again and took a deep breath before opening his eyes and looking at Emily. "You say that, but I sense a connection. You've been drawn to Torquay because of him."

"Well, I heard he might be in danger."

"So you really are a private investigator!"

"Not really. In my day job I do office administration."

"What sort of danger is he in? Robbery? He wouldn't bring the fifty grand here with him, surely?"

"Not robbery. Drowning. It might not be him. But I'm supposed to make a report on it. A few psychics have been getting premonitions."

Bobby did his eye-closing, deep-breathing routine again. When he opened his eyes again, he shook his head. "I'm not getting anything. If they pick up any clues, the dogs'll tell me and I'll tell you. Shirley's my best communicator."

"Thank you." Emily took her notebook from her handbag. She wrote the names of Bobby's dogs in it. "Do you think you can win the challenge?"

"Honestly? I don't see Edmund Zenon handing over the cash to anyone, do you? He's gone around for years saying there's no such thing as the supernatural. So how's he going to stand there tomorrow and say, OK, I was wrong?"

"But you're still going to do the challenge?"

"I want the chance to show what I can do. The people who believe will believe. If they've heard I've signed up for this, they'll come and find me after. It's a roundabout way of establishing my credentials, because you can't sign up without getting vetted. I hope it'll help with bookings." He shrugged, slightly embarrassed. "There must be better ways to earn a living. But this is my calling."

"What about the other people here? Do you know any of them?"

Bobby looked around the public rooms of the hotel, most of which were open plan, the various areas differentiated by contrasting decorative themes and styles of seating. The dogs noticed him looking. They perked up and looked around, too. In the library, the lobby, the bar and the restaurant, there were individuals sitting quietly, going over notes, frowning and annotating the margins of speeches. Others had gathered in huddles, whispering and planning, laughing and talking. The place was so crowded, it was difficult for Emily and Bobby to get a good look at anything other than the buttons on the jackets of the people standing a few feet in front of them.

"There are some dangerous people here," said Bobby.

"Who? Can you point them out to me?"

"I don't know them. I feel them. Do you have a weapon?"

"No!"

Bobby's dogs bared their teeth. Shirley began growling.

"Well, never mind."

"Why do you think I need a weapon?"

"If someone wants to get to Edmund Zenon and you've been asking questions . . . I mean, I know everything about what you're doing here, and we've only been talking for five minutes. And that's without using my powers. You can trust me, but I can't say the same for others here."

"OK, good tip. I'll try to be discreet."

Bobby stood up as Shirley growled again. "You tell Jessie to keep close and watch out for you."

"I don't . . . I mean, Jessie was a lovely dog. But she's gone now. I don't think I can talk to her."

"We don't know what we can do till we're tested. If you're in danger, you try telling Jessie to get a message to Shirley and if she can do it, Shirley will tell me and we'll come running. Meantime, I better take this lot out for a walk. Being inside with all the bad vibrations is making them antsy." He stood and arranged the dogs so their leads wouldn't tangle up with each other.

"Bobby, if a dead person could send a message to help me—or Edmund Zenon for that matter—why would they do that when they could have sent messages to stop thousands of people being killed in all the wars over the years?"

"P'raps they did, and people just didn't listen." Bobby raised his neatly groomed eyebrows at Emily and smiled, then he walked away with his dachshunds. Tails held high, the dogs' glossy chestnut fur rippled and swished, as gorgeous as the glossy chestnut curls of a pulp fiction pinup walking away from the hero in the final scene.

There were no walls or doorways separating the hotel restaurant from the lobby, just an assortment of comfortable chairs and sofas forming a café/bar area. Peeking through the crowd in the lobby, and beyond that to the bar, and beyond that to the Riviera Lounge, Emily glimpsed Gerald sitting at one of the restaurant's tables by a picture window, looking out at the sea.

As she headed in his direction, the woman with gray-blonde hair and rosy complexion stepped forward and intercepted her. "Excuse me? I'm Sarah Taylor. Could I talk to you? I'm sitting over here with my husband, Tim, and our friend Joseph Seppardi."

Sarah pointed as she said their names. Tim was a tall man. He put his hand up and smoothed his dark hair, even though it didn't need taming; a quick, tentative movement that looked as though he was patting his head to check the top of it wasn't missing. Joseph Seppardi was a sinister-looking man, alert and watchful, clasping the arms of his chair like a bird of prey gripping its perch.

"We saw you talking to that chap in the blue suit. Is he a psychic?"

Emily hadn't signed a confidentiality agreement, but she didn't want to give away any of Bobby's secrets. She decided to be cagey, until she knew more. "I was admiring his dachshunds."

Sarah looked embarrassed when she realized Emily wasn't going to confide in her. "I wondered if you'd lost someone. I thought if the man with the dogs couldn't help you . . . Well, Joseph's been very good to us, with our Liam."

"That's nice of you, but I'm OK. Are you here to take part in the challenge?"

Sarah scratched at her arm. She glanced over at her husband and their friend. "Joseph's going to do it."

Emily paused to consider what she should say, under the circumstances. *Good luck* didn't sound right. He wasn't taking his driving test. *I'm sure he'll do well* wasn't quite truthful. She said, "Well, it would be amazing if he could prove the existence of the paranormal."

"We know it exists. We're not here for that. We're here for the money." She lowered her voice. "And to put Edmund Zenon in his place."

CHAPTER SEVEN
THE POSITIVITY CIRCLE

By the time Emily reached Gerald in the Riviera Lounge, Peg was there too, a pale green paisley scarf pinned to her shoulder and a hardback book in her hand. Dr. Muriel was just behind Emily—she could hear her friend calling out greetings to delegates as she made her way to the table. Gerald had ordered club sandwiches for all four of them, and the waiter brought their plates to the table just as Emily sat down.

Gerald leaned across the table with his phone in his hand. "Anything to report? Anything I can put on Twitter?"

Emily put some mayonnaise on her plate and dipped one of her French fries in it. "I need to talk to Edmund. I haven't had much luck so far."

Peg smiled. "You know what, dear? Sometimes it's easier to talk to the dead than the living. You want to come along to my positivity circle this afternoon? It's in the Winston Churchill room. You, too, Muriel. We're looking for intelligent, open-minded women."

"Ha!" said Dr. Muriel. "I'm afraid I'll have to pass on that. I've some work to do on my talk for tomorrow."

"Have you had any more messages?" Emily asked Peg.

"No. Though I haven't been tuning in to the other world. I've been busy setting up my book stall."

"You're not planning to sell your books here, are you?" said Gerald.

"Course not!" said Peg. "I've no *intention* of selling. Though I expect I shall have to supply one or two copies in exchange for money if people ask for them." She winked at Emily.

While Gerald tried to think of a way to close down Peg's commercial activities without offending her, Emily asked the same question she had asked Bobby. "Why would a ghost or a spirit send back a message about Edmund Zenon? There must be so many other tragedies they could try to prevent."

"My premonition isn't from a dead person," said Peg. "This is from someone living."

"Is it?" said Gerald. "But I do think Lady Lacey was interested in messages from the spirit world. At the time of her death she was a spiritualist."

"Was she?" said Peg innocently. "I looked over the documents and she didn't specify."

"Do you mean you got a phone call from someone about the drowning?" asked Emily.

"No, dear. Telepathy."

Emily wiped her hands and got out her notebook. "So is it the murderer broadcasting their intentions, do you think, or is it someone else, trying to warn you?"

"I don't know. I can get a very good telepathic connection with the living—but they have to be prepared to let me in. From what I saw of it, I was dealing with a disturbed mind, and most of it was closed to me. Couldn't tell you if it was a man or a woman, even."

"If the person's here in Torquay, will the messages be stronger than they were in London now that you're here, too?"

"Could be. I shall have to have a session this afternoon, see what I can see."

"I suppose it wouldn't make any difference to the strength of the signal if the person was in London yesterday and is in Torquay today," said Gerald. "If they've remained roughly the same distance from you?"

"Good point!" said Emily. She scribbled a few notes.

"You seem more convinced than you were yesterday, Emily," said Dr. Muriel. "Excited, even."

"I'm not sure if I believe in ghosts and spirits. No offense, Peg."

"None taken, dear."

"But I think I believe in telepathy. It ought to be possible for someone to pick up a message like this from another living person, if it's broadcast strongly enough. Shouldn't it? And a murder—the intention of murder—would send a very strong signal."

"Edmund Zenon says not," said Dr. Muriel.

Peg's hand went to the brooch at her shoulder. "I don't know what it is with magicians. They make a living out of tricking people—they think everyone's at it."

"If something like this were to be proved," Emily asked, "would it win the challenge?"

"Oh, I shouldn't want the money!" said Peg virtuously.

"You wouldn't need it," said Gerald. "You'd be famous."

◆ ◆ ◆

Sarah, Tim and Joseph Seppardi took a seat at the next table. Sarah nodded at Emily, picked up the menu and began fussing. "Would you like the mushroom quiche or the risotto, Tim? Or how about the chicken breast with potatoes? You might like that. Or the Thai fish cakes. You need some fiber in your diet. You know what the doctor said. Will you have the fish cakes? What about you, Joe?"

"I'll have the fish cakes," Tim said.

Joseph Seppardi said, "I'm not sure if this is the right thing for us to do."

"You don't want the fish cakes?" Sarah was flustered.

"What you're proposing . . . the challenge. Is it what Liam would want?"

"Is he here?" Sarah yelped. "Is Liam with us?"

A few heads turned. Everyone at Emily's table stopped talking and listened.

"I've been thinking about it," Tim said, "and I think we should build something in memory of Liam."

Sarah ignored him. She was looking at Joseph.

"He's not here," Joseph told her.

Tim started talking like a contestant on a radio show who has been told he mustn't pause or hesitate, or he will forfeit his turn. "Liam used to like making things, didn't he, Sarah, when he was about seven or eight years old? We could build a science block in a school or something. There's the money we'd put away in case Liam wanted to study. A deposit for a flat when he got married. We could use that."

Joseph seemed unenthusiastic. "If only the planning regulations weren't so absurd these days."

Tim began arguing with himself about the plans for the science block. "We need to have something we could look at, and everyone will know what it is. I'd like to build something. But I don't know what they'd say if we turned up at the school wanting something named after him. Remember that fuss with the explosives in the boys' toilets?"

"We don't have enough money, Tim." Sarah picked up a fork and turned it over in her hand, then she scratched at her arm with it, distractedly. "But we could build something without bricks. A foundation. We're here to fight for what we believe in—for what Joe believes in. If we had a foundation, we could help other people who are bereaved. What do you say to that, eh, Tim? The Joseph Seppardi Foundation."

"It sounds expensive," said Tim. "The administration. No end to it. No exit strategy. At least if you build something, you lay the last brick and you're done. With this, I don't know . . . How would we fund it? If we ran out of money, we'd have to turn people away. We'd have to charge a fee."

Sarah put the fork down. "I wouldn't want to charge a fee."

Tim sighed. He pushed his glasses higher up on the bridge of his nose. He gave the top of his head a quick pat to check it was still there. "If we could double our money, we could build something really special. Maybe a school. You know, I feel like a man wandering around with half a winning lottery ticket. What we have just isn't enough."

"Gambling isn't the answer," said Joseph Seppardi.

"Nobody's talking about gambling," Sarah said. "You're supposed to win the fifty thousand pounds. It's why Liam brought us here. What kind of charitable project he wants it spent on, we can clarify after."

"Can we, though?" Tim asked her. "You know what he was like, even . . . I mean, I wouldn't put it beyond him to, you know . . . He liked a joke. That business with the English teacher's car, and then the explosion. He could be mischievous. So . . ."

The people at Emily's table paid Tim more attention than Sarah did. Eventually he trailed off. He touched the top of his head. No, still there. He picked up his glass of water and took a sip.

"If you win the money, Joe, you can have your foundation." Sarah glanced at Emily's table. Everyone looked down at their plates, pretending they weren't listening.

"I don't want a foundation," said Joseph Seppardi.

Sarah spoke quietly, but her words were audible. "Imagine taking the magician's money and using it against him."

"We could call it the Robin Hood Foundation," said Tim, cheering up a bit.

"Let's not call it that," said Sarah.

Joseph Seppardi said nothing, but he looked miserable.

The fish cakes arrived. The three of them tucked into their meal.

◆ ◆ ◆

"What's everyone up to this afternoon?" Gerald asked the group at his table as he signaled the waiter for the bill. They were on the coffee now.

"I'm going to spend some time in my positivity circle, see if we can't send some protection Edmund Zenon's way," said Peg.

"Ah," said Gerald, "but how will you know who to protect him from?"

"We'll send out general positivity, Gerald, to avert the malice." Peg spoke as though Gerald was a buffoon for not knowing how positivity circles worked.

Emily took a cube of brown sugar from the sugar bowl and stirred it into her coffee. "If he's in danger, could it be from someone who's nowhere near the conference: they're upset they're not invited and they're just *thinking* about throttling Edmund—they won't do it?"

Gerald spread his hands in a gesture that took in the whole of Torquay. "Everyone's here. Even people who haven't been invited."

"Besides, wouldn't they be thinking about throttling Gerald for not inviting them?" asked Dr. Muriel. "Or Peg? She's invited the psychics to this event."

Peg put her fingers to her throat. She stroked the skin thoughtfully and looked over at Joseph Seppardi. "You know what'd worry me? If we had someone here who was under the control of a mischievous spirit. That would be alarming. Very alarming."

"Fortunately Emily's here to investigate," said Dr. Muriel. "To future crimes!" She clinked her coffee cup against Emily's, attracting the attention of some of the other people in the restaurant, including the party at the next table.

Still anxious about the conference—and perhaps a bit miffed at Dr. Muriel's refusal to take Emily's preparation of the report seriously—Gerald stood up to leave. The others followed suit. Peg picked up the copy of *Psychic Techniques for Future Positivity* she had brought in with her and stopped to talk to Sarah as she passed her table. "I don't mean to interrupt. I'm putting together a circle of positivity in the Winston Churchill room. Strong, intelligent, spiritual women. Would you like to join us?"

"Oh, no. I mean, you know . . ." Sarah looked at Joseph for permission.

"I think you should go," said Tim. "Do you good to make some friends. I'll go for a walk along the sea front. Stretch my legs."

Sarah said to Peg, "I don't think I can join you. I need to spend this afternoon trying to get through to our son, Liam."

"Did you need a pathway into the spirit world?"

"How did you know he'd died?" Sarah was impressed.

"It's either that or he's having trouble with his mobile phone. Since you're at a hotel where matters of a paranormal nature will be discussed, and since you're with a spiritualist gentleman who clearly has been gifted with psychic powers"— Joseph Seppardi nodded his head in acknowledgment of this bit of toadying—"Well, let's just call it a lucky guess." Peg smiled broadly, to show that the last bit was a joke. She was someone who *knew* things. She never had to guess.

Emily saw that Sarah was disarmed. Joseph Seppardi wasn't.

"Joe's been helping us with Liam. But I s'pose there's no harm in getting a second opinion. Is there, Joe? I mean, when we thought Tim had bowel cancer, when he had blood in his—"

Peg nodded vigorously. "Of course, dear. You just want to do what's best for Liam."

"Yes."

"You come along to my positivity circle and we'll talk about it. Here you are. You better have a copy of my book."

"Thank you." Sarah reached for the copy of *Future Positivity* that Peg held out to her.

"Twelve ninety-nine in the shops but you can have one now for ten pounds, and I'll sign it for you. What name shall I write in it?"

Emily could see that Sarah didn't want a copy of Peg's book. But she did want to talk to Liam. "Sarah," she said.

As they walked out of the restaurant, Peg put her hand on Emily's arm so she would drop back behind Gerald and Dr. Muriel, who were walking on ahead. "Big favor. Can you hold the fort in the Winston Churchill room for five minutes while I pop out and do something? If anyone comes asking for my positivity circle, I don't want them finding the room empty."

"What are you popping out for?" Emily knew very well that five minutes was one of those elastic measures of time that could be anything from five minutes to an hour, depending on who was speaking and who was listening. And as for popping out, that could mean anything. She had heard of errant husbands popping out for a pint of milk and a packet of cigarettes and not being seen for twenty-five years.

"I'm not going far. I need to make a call to the features editor of the *Sunday Sentinel*."

Peg went to make her call. Emily went to the Winston Churchill room. There was a circle of chairs set up, and a table with a display of Peg's books. Emily picked one up, turned it over and looked at the blurb on the back. The author photo showed a youngish black-and-white Peg looking pensive, her chin propped on her fist.

"Am I early?" It was Sarah. She walked warily past the display of books, as if she thought she might have to buy another one if she got too close. She sat on one of the chairs outside the circle. Then she got up and sat on a chair inside the circle.

"Peg'll be back in a minute." As a measurement of time, a minute was even more elastic than five minutes.

"I don't know if I'm doing the right thing, doing this. Joseph's been so good to us."

"Helping you talk to Liam?"

"See, that's the thing. Liam's not saying anything. He's gone missing since we've come to Torquay. Sounds odd to say it like that. How do you track down a dead boy? I can hardly call the police. Tim says he's at peace now."

"Perhaps he is."

Sarah shook her head. "I think it's something to do with Edmund Zenon. He's scared."

"Edmund?"

Sarah gawped at her. "What's Edmund got to be scared of?"

Women began drifting into the room and taking their places in the circle. They were dressed in vibrant, life-affirming colors, with swirly skirts and headscarves. They had tinted hair and wore silver rings and bangles, dressed in a way that ought to have emphasized their individuality—Emily rarely saw people looking like that on the tube in London during the morning commute—yet they all looked remarkably similar.

When there were a dozen of them in the room, with no more drifting in, Peg returned from making her call, shut the door and walked inside the circle. She spoke to the group with friendly, confident charm. It was impossible to dislike her. Not that Emily was trying.

"We're here today because I have had a premonition. A man drowning. Anyone else getting that? Dreams, visions, tea leaves or cards?"

Some of the women nodded.

"There's dark forces gathered in Torquay." Peg closed her eyes and held her hands out in front of her, as if holding back these dark forces. "I want you to bring to mind a man named Edmund Zenon. Find something bright in your hearts. Use it to put a force around him, to protect him. Whatever darkness comes for him, we want to deflect it. We want it to bounce off like a bullet bouncing off a shield."

As she slipped out of the room, Emily had the horrible thought that if Peg's shield did work, the darkness that was meant for Edmund might bounce off and hurt someone else by mistake. She was being fanciful; it was the atmosphere in the hotel. She would go and take a few lungfuls of the fresh air that Dr. Muriel set so much store by, and then sit somewhere quiet to get her thoughts in order so she could write up some notes in her notebook.

The hotel entrance was quiet now that Edmund had made his appearance. There were no protestors, no bystanders. The lobby was still crowded, but it was easy to spot Tim Taylor walking out through the glass doors because he was taller than most of the people in the room.

Emily hurried to catch up with him. She asked him if he was heading into town.

"Just going to stretch my legs. How'd the positivity circle go? Was Sarah there?"

"Yes. I left them to it."

"You didn't want to join in?"

"I don't think I really believe in it. I'd feel a bit of a phony joining in. You know?"

Emily and Tim crossed the road together and began to walk downhill toward the town, along a path with a road on their left and the sea to their right. It was just after two o'clock, but the light was poor; it felt more like evening than afternoon. The sea was choppy and gray, the tide was high. There was a low wall running along the side of the path, with railings on top of it and gaps at regular intervals to allow access to steps leading down to the beach below. Further down the beach, toward the town center, a small crowd had gathered, though Emily and Tim weren't close enough to see what was happening down there. Behind them, the hotel was on top of a hill at one side of the bay. The path sloped gently downward until it reached the town center and the harbor in the middle of the bay, where it was almost level with the sea, and then it began to climb again to the top of the cliff at the other side.

The wind coming in from the sea was cold, and Emily turned up her collar to keep the chill off her face. "I'm sorry to hear about your son," she said. It was all she needed to say for Tim to start talking as they walked down the hill.

His hand went to his hair. He brushed his fingertips across the top of his head. "Thanks. I've been feeling a bit sorry for myself, too, since it happened. There's this awkwardness with people at work. My boss, my colleagues—people I used to enjoy a pint of beer or a game of golf with—they're sympathetic, but what I'm going through is beyond their understanding. Have you ever lost someone close like that?"

"No."

"I have less in common with my friends than I once did. It's a lonely feeling. You start to feel like an outsider. You feel a kinship with other outsiders, no matter what put them there. You start to look for those people. You get people who say they want to help. Sometimes you feel hugely grateful to them. Other times you feel resentful. You don't know who to trust. You feel emotional. That's not me. Or it wasn't."

They walked to the next set of steps going down to the beach from the path. Now they were close enough to get a good look at what was going on below them. A group of people were listening to a man who was standing up to his calves at the edge of the water. The man was in his mid to late fifties. He had close-cropped, gray hair and a handsome, suntanned face. He was wearing a billowing white shirt, his trousers rolled up to his knees, and he was shouting . . . No, he was preaching. No, he was singing!

"Dear Lord and father of mankind, forgive our foolish ways . . ."

"My favorite hymn!" said Tim. "You know, I never really thought about it before. It's about God being a father."

He left Emily and walked down the steps leading to the beach. As he reached the edge of the crowd, he joined in singing the beautiful hymn. Emily stood and watched him for a few minutes, then she carried on walking into town.

CHAPTER EIGHT
CUP O' ROSIE

As Emily was passing the Fly Me to the Moon travel agency just off the High Street, it started to rain. Colorful posters on the walls inside advertised enticing destinations and experiences. Wouldn't she rather be on a Nile cruise in Egypt, admiring the Toblerone chunks of honeycomb-yellow pyramids against the forever blue of a sunny sky? Or standing in a forest in Norway, reaching for the ungraspable firework beauty of the northern lights in the night sky? Or riding on an elephant in India, protected by a parasol as pink and exotic as a maharani's painted toenails?

For the stay-at-home adventurer, there was another alternative. Fixed to the window, no less colorful or enticing than any of the other pictures, a poster depicted Edmund Zenon in his scarlet-lined black cape and his black top hat, balancing on a glassy green sea, arms outstretched against a blue sky that faded to a pink horizon. Torquay. Easter weekend. Who could fail to be excited when they saw that?

Emily was excited. But it was raining and she had to keep walking. The Cup O' Rosie tea shop was next door to the travel agency, offering customers warmth and a break from the rainy English weather at a fraction of the price of a Nile cruise. Emily peered into the dingy "olde-worlde" interior, wondering whether she was thirsty, when an attractive, fair-haired man of about thirty stood up from a table near the window and started waving at her. She went inside.

She had met Chris on bonfire night in November the year before. A ragtag troupe of circus performers and avant-garde entertainers had taken over a big empty house at the end of the street where Emily and Dr. Muriel lived. They had thrown a memorable party. Chris had been their leader; an anticapitalist activist. Was he here to disrupt the conference?

Chris looked embarrassed. "Actually, no. I woke up one day and realized I was sick."

"Oh!"

He shrugged and smiled, to show that he had been making a joke. "Sick of being poor. Sick of looking out for everyone and no one looking after me. I don't know if I've done the right thing coming down here. It was all a bit last minute. But if you don't do something with your life, you're never going to find out if you'll regret it."

"What might you regret?"

"Have you heard of Edmund Zenon? The magician?"

"Don't tell me! You've got a hundred masked stilt-walkers converging on Torquay to juggle fire in front of the Hotel Majestic tomorrow, in protest against his paranormal challenge."

"Sounds great! If I ever get back into agitprop theater, I'll give you a call. No, I'm down here because Ed's got a big performance set up. His usual guy had to go abroad at short notice. I've taken the corporate coin, Emily. I'm working as Edmund Zenon's technical advisor."

"The other guy ditched him right before a big event?"

Chris shrugged. "Had a better offer. Interview for a job in Rio. They want him to get involved in the opening ceremony for the next Olympic Games. Who's gonna say no to that?"

Emily wondered what the poster would look like, if the absentee technical advisor's prospective employers had decided to entice him to Rio with an image rather than an email or a phone call. It would probably have the famous Art Deco statue of Christ the Redeemer on it, arms outstretched atop the Corcovado mountain, his embrace taking in the city of Rio below him. If it came down to a fight for possession of the technical advisor, would it be the white-robed statue standing on the mountain, or the black-clothed magician standing on the waves in Torquay who would win?

Chris misinterpreted her silence. "Ed won't find anyone better than me. He's in safe hands." Still prickly. Still arrogant. Still handsome, too. With his messy blond hair, his battered blue jeans and his chunky, fisherman's rib sweater, he looked like a mail-order boyfriend. Except for his sardonic smile.

Emily ordered a pot of tea.

"Why are *you* here, Emily?"

Should she mention the future crimes investigations? The paranormal dog? Lady Lacey Carmichael's tragic losses in the First World War? "I'm on holiday."

"Really?" He tilted his head slightly, as if looking at her from an angle would make it easier to see if she was lying.

It didn't feel like a lie. She *was* enjoying herself—and she wasn't the only one. Groups of local teenagers were sitting together, gossiping and planning, the flickering electric candlelight from the lamps on the tables picking out the excitement on their faces. A famous magician was in town! She could hear them talking about Ouija boards and card tricks, and what they would do if they won fifty thousand pounds.

A pale girl with black, spiky hair and great flicks of black eyeliner on her eyelids had torn the cellophane wrapper off a pack of tarot cards and was peering at the instructions, following the lines of print with a forefinger decorated with black nail varnish. "What's the card for drowning?"

"What's the obsession with drowning round here?" Chris asked Emily. "It's all anyone talks about. Beware the water! Don't go into the sea! It's like we're the only two sane people in a village of web-footed crazies, cursed by the sea witch."

Emily laughed. "Who else has been talking about drowning?"

"Who *hasn't*? There's some kind of prediction going round about Ed, apparently. We've got this really complicated trick . . . Well, you know what? I'm not gonna be one of those men who talk about themselves all the time. What have *you* been up to, Emily? You look great."

Emily's dilemma was that she didn't want Chris to be one of those men who talk about themselves all the time, either. But she did want him to talk about Edmund Zenon.

"I think it's only a problem if men talk about themselves when they're on a first date."

"I guess we'd go somewhere more exciting if we were on a date."

Emily would have liked to ask where they might have gone on a date. But she had a report to write. Back to business. "A really complicated trick sounds interesting."

"I'd better not say. It's a kind of immersive theater—"

"Immersive? Like . . . drowning?"

Chris laughed. "I've only been here twenty-four hours and now I'm at it! OK, it's like street theater, only bigger and better. Well, if you know anything about Ed, you'd know everything with him has to be bigger and better."

"I don't know anything about him. I'd like to meet him."

"Yeah?" There was something in the way he said it—was it jealousy?—that made Emily wonder why Chris had taken this job.

Actually, Emily had met Edmund, briefly. She corrected herself. "Well, I did meet him this morning, but I didn't get the chance to talk to him. He checked into my friend's room at the Hotel Majestic."

"What do you mean? How can he be staying in your friend's room?"

"The receptionist gave him my friend's room by mistake. Said she thought she'd been hypnotized." They both laughed at that. "It's strange to see you here, working for Edmund Zenon. I can't imagine you taking orders from him."

"Taking orders? I'm not the butler." That sardonic smile, then a shrug. "The work'll be interesting. I'll learn something. Can't say better than that, can you? Then, sooner or later, I'll move on."

The volume and intensity of teenage chatter increased as a mysterious, tragic-looking woman in a dark purple mohair coat and sunglasses came into the shop. She looked around, her eyes adjusting to the gloom, and then she came over to Emily. She gripped the back of an empty chair at their table, leaning forward. "You've got a lucky face. I'll read your palm."

Emily didn't believe you could be cursed by a fortune-teller. But she wished the woman would go away. "No thanks."

But the woman didn't go away. She took off her sunglasses and looked at Emily steadily. Emily looked back, unafraid, to show that she was not superstitious. The woman had an interesting face. She had good bone structure, with sharp cheekbones and brown-green lily-pond eyes. But the corners of her lips turned down, as if she had tried one day to fly off and leave her cares behind, and cruel fingers had reached up and hooked onto her mouth to keep her earthbound.

"I'll do it for nothing. For luck."

"Here! You can do mine." Chris put out his hand and smiled reassuringly at Emily, like an older brother breaking a chain letter. Emily wasn't sure whether to be irritated or charmed.

"You want me to tell you if you'll be lucky in love?" The fortune-teller stroked the palm of Chris's hand with the pad of her thumb very gently. Chris shivered. The woman spoke teasingly. "Maybe I shouldn't tell you."

"No, go on."

"You won't be lucky in love. Not this time."

Chris smiled a wry little smile.

"You're going on a long journey. Overseas."

This was too much for some of the teenagers nearby who had been watching, fascinated. One of them called over, "Yeah, but get to it. Is anyone going to drown?"

The fortune-teller seemed to ignore the disruption. But her next words thrilled the watching teens. "Are you afraid of the water, Chris?"

"No."

"You work on the water?"

"Not exactly, no."

The fortune-teller kept hold of Chris's hand, but she no longer looked at it. She looked into his eyes. "You have an important job to do—you've come a long way to do it. It's connected to water. Listen to me because I have an important job to do, too. I have to give you a warning. Keep away from the water this weekend."

Everyone was listening now—Emily, Chris, the assembled teenagers, the tourists, the waitress, the cook, the owner of the tea shop. The fortune-teller in the mohair coat held onto the silence. Emily's neighbor Victoria, who had earned her living as an actress and now ran a stage school for children, had once told Emily that the rule in the theater is that you can *always* hold onto a silence longer than you think you can, if you have the audience's attention. So you should just go for it. Chris had spent his whole adult life performing, albeit in circus shows and street theater. He also knew how to hold on to silence. And when it was time for the silence to end, he knew how to feed a lady her line.

"Why do I need to keep away from water?"

"Because something bad is going to happen. Someone is going to drown."

The fortune-teller straightened and let go of Chris's hand. She walked out of the tea shop slowly and gracefully, without looking back.

The teenagers giggled and chattered excitedly.

"You don't believe in it, do you?" Emily asked Chris. She was feeling a bit spooked.

"No, I don't."

"So how did she know your name was Chris?"

"Cor!" said one of the teenagers. "She knew his name!"

"She knew his name! She knew his name!" The buzz went round in respectful, frightened whispers until one of the teenagers started laughing. Then everything started up again, as though the tea shop had been momentarily frozen in time, and had only needed the sound of a child's laughter to break the spell and return to normal. The teenagers went back to talking about Edmund Zenon and how they would spend his money if they won it. The waitress took her notepad out of her apron and went to a table to take an order. The cook went back in the kitchen, and the tea shop owner got on the phone and called *everybody* to tell them what had just happened.

"You know her!" Emily said to Chris. "That's the only explanation."

"Is it?" Chris laughed. He checked the time on his mobile phone. "I'm supposed to be meeting Ed at the Smell of a Book bookshop on the High Street. Want to come with me?"

"Isn't he doing a talk? I saw a poster for it when I arrived at the station. I'd rather meet him when there aren't lots of people around him."

"The talk should be over now. We'll catch him on his way back to the hotel."

On the short walk from the tea shop to the bookshop, Emily saw two posters advertising Edmund's *Don't Believe the Hype* book.

The image was the same one he had used on the other posters. All around town, she had seen the same thing: Edmund Zenon in top hat and cape, arms outstretched, floating above the water, his feet just touching the waves.

"What do you see when you look at those posters?" Chris asked her.

"I see . . . adventure, mystery, intrigue. What do you see?"

He shrugged. "I see a businessman who's got rich by dressing up as an entertainer."

When they arrived at the bookshop, it was packed. The talk was so popular that the start time had been delayed by half an hour as everyone squeezed in. Emily had no chance of a quiet chat alone with Edmund. She could just about see him across the room, dressed expensively but unshowily in a good pair of jeans and a black cashmere sweater.

The mayor was there, the town crier was there; both in their chains of office, livery and tricorn hats, the mayor with his mace and the town crier with his handbell. Alice and Ben were there—the couple from the train. Ben noticed Emily and gave her a thumbs-up. There were more men than women in the audience, several of them wearing black T-shirts with *I Believe . . . in Edmund Zenon* printed on the front. They applauded enthusiastically when Edmund was introduced. He began with a joke.

"Now, I've got to tell you, I've just had a quiet word with the manager. I noticed some of these books on the subject of nutrition have been wrongly shelved. Should be over there with the rest of the fiction."

Several people in the crowd tittered.

Edmund held up his hands. "Look, it isn't just the idea that the food you eat can make a difference to your health that's wrong. My book covers all sorts of delusions. Today I'm going to talk a little bit about faith. Someone came up to me after one of my Don't Believe the Hype gigs in London the other day."

"Yo!" said Ben, to let everyone else know he had been there. He put up his hand to adjust his knitted hat and his jacket kinked open. He was wearing an *I Believe* T-shirt.

"This woman told me her faith gives her strength. You hear people say that faith itself is what's important, not whether what they believe is true. But you need to have faith in *yourself.* Not God. Not the Prophet or Jehovah. Don't be a dupe."

"Too right. Global conspiracy!" someone shouted from near the front. "What about Palestine?"

"I said *dupe*," said Edmund Zenon sharply. "Don't be a dupe."

Chris rolled his eyes at Emily and edged back through the door, holding it open so she could follow him. But Emily decided to stay and listen. During Edmund's talk, which lasted for around fifteen minutes, Emily learned that he disapproved of everything that could possibly give anyone any comfort or relief, whether physical or emotional. If she wanted to make a list of his potential enemies, she might as well just write down *everyone*. Edmund was charming and he spoke eloquently, without notes. But there was something empty in his message. Emily wondered why it mattered so much to him what other people believed. She remembered what Peg had said about magicians seeing trickery everywhere because they used trickery themselves.

"If you take homeopathic medicine or flower remedies, if you pray to God or cross the road when you see a black cat, if you go to church or the mosque or the synagogue, if you eat yoghurt because you think it will make your digestive system healthy, if you take vitamin C because you think it will prevent the onset of the common cold, then you're kidding yourself. Don't believe the hype!"

"Mind you," whispered a woman standing next to Emily, "vitamin C does help if you take it in big doses at the first sign of a cold. And as for yoghurt—"

"Can you hear me at the back?" called Edmund.

"Ooh, yes! Thank you!" said the woman. And then, quiet enough for only Emily to hear, "But hearing isn't the same as believing, is it?"

"I wish he'd do some tricks," whispered Emily. "I love close-up magic."

"Shhh!" one of the men in black T-shirts said.

A table at the side of the room had been stacked with books so Edmund could sign them after his talk was finished. Judging by the size of the crowd, he would be there for at least another hour, with no chance of Emily getting to talk to him alone. She decided to leave him to it and go back to the hotel.

CHAPTER NINE
PLEDGE AND PLUNGE

On her way back to the hotel, Emily passed a shop in the High Street called A Little of What You Fancy. It must have been the only shop in Torquay that didn't have one of Edmund's posters in the window. A postcard-sized sign said MADAME NOVA WILL TELL YOUR FORTUNE. BY APPOINTMENT ONLY. Emily saw wands, capes, wings, wigs and moustaches on display. A sign in the middle of the door said, SORRY! NOW CLOSED FOR LUNCH. At four o'clock? Emily pushed at the door, just in case, but it didn't open.

She walked past the tourist office. She walked past a shop called Faith & Hope—and she stopped outside when she saw yet another poster in the window: Edmund Zenon walking on water, of course. Why were all these people so keen to put up posters advertising . . . advertising what, exactly? Edmund Zenon's presence in Torquay. Big deal. It was as if he'd taken over their minds! Emily peered into the shop and saw that Faith & Hope was a charity shop that collected and sold books, clothes and bric-a-brac on behalf of the local hospice. There were two customers she recognized as Hilary and Trina, the woman and teenage girl who had been holding the placards outside the hotel.

She opened the door and went inside. "Hello!" she said, as if people from London always called out a cheery greeting when they went into a shop.

The volunteer behind the till nodded. Hilary and Trina looked round but they didn't acknowledge her. Emily went and stood by a shelf of VHS videos, positioning herself so she could see what they were up to. Hilary was browsing the racks of fungal-smelling second-hand clothes, watched closely by the volunteer. She held up a pink, strappy sundress against herself. "This one, Trina?"

"Urgh. I don't want a dress," Trina said. "Hilary!"

Emily caught Trina's eye and smiled.

"Well, you need *something*. This one?" Hilary held up a white, voluminous sundress. "Trina? This one?"

Trina scowled and fanned her hand in front of her nose. "This place stinks."

The volunteer was offended, as well she might be. She looked at Emily for sympathy. But Emily pretended to be fascinated by a *Fawlty Towers* video.

The doorbell jangled again. Emily, Trina and Hilary looked round to see a woman wearing an expensive-looking dark purple mohair coat and sunglasses. The fortune-teller. She was carrying a stack of books and a folded-up dress in a large carrier bag with "A Little of What You Fancy" printed on it in cursive script. At first she didn't see that there were customers in the shop—those dark glasses couldn't be helping much.

When she noticed she wasn't alone, the fortune-teller looked startled—frightened, even. She took a step backwards. Emily wasn't sure who had provoked this reaction? Hilary? Trina? Emily? Was she frightened of all three of them?

"Hello!" said Emily in her friendliest tone. The fortune-teller took another step back.

The volunteer put out her hands to accept the donations. She spoke cheerily, as if it wasn't unusual for a customer to behave as if she had fallen through a wormhole into the wrong dimension, only to be faced with three of her deadliest foes. "Madame Nova! What-ever did you say to Jackie Churchill and her bridesmaids last night?

My Larry heard them talking about it in the Lamb and Dragon on the High Street after!"

"You'll know what I said, then, if you heard it from Larry," said Madame Nova, regaining her poise.

"Drowning, though! Was that it? You said something about one of them drowning? You didn't mean it?" The volunteer put out her hands again, coaxingly.

Madame Nova took a step closer to the till. She handed over her bag of clothes. "I was having some fun with the girls. I hardly remember what I said."

Hilary had been listening to this. "You were trying to warn them about something? What did you think was going to happen?"

"Just having a little fun," Madame Nova said, without looking at Hilary. She nodded to the woman at the till and left the shop.

"Whoa!" Trina's black-painted eyes were wide as a Disney princess's.

"She said something about drowning to me just now," Emily said, hoping she wasn't going to get ignored again. "Well, she said it to my friend. We were having tea in the tea shop down there, and she came in and read his palm."

"She never!" Trina said, fascinated. Emily was struck by the similarity in age of this girl and the teenagers in the Cup O' Rosie—and how carefree they were, and how pinch-faced and pale this girl was. "She say *how* it'll happen?"

Hilary gave the white sundress on its hanger to Trina and motioned that she should take it up to the till. "No one's going to drown."

"I don't believe in it," said Emily. "But she was quite convincing. She warned my friend not to go into the water."

Hilary whirled round, almost tripping over two overstuffed plastic bags at her feet. "It's not dangerous to go into the water, if you do it for the right reasons." She picked up the bags and went to the till to pay for the sundress.

There was an orange candlewick bedspread rolled up and stuffed into each bag. The volunteer put her hands out for them, assuming they were donations. "You want me to take those for you?"

"Thank you, no. I'm afraid we'll be needing them." Hilary paid for the sundress and left the shop, Trina following after her.

"Something's going to happen," said the volunteer to Emily. "You can feel it—all the kids are excited. Not just because they're off for the holidays. There's a festival feel in town. I dunno what's going to happen but it's got to be something good, hasn't it, if it's to do with that magician."

Emily, freshly arrived from the metropolis, thought that if teenagers congregating in a tea shop trying to do magic tricks passed for a "festival feel" in Torquay, then she wouldn't want to be here when the town was experiencing a slump. "What about all this talk about drowning?"

"That's just Madame Nova. She's got the shop next door but one. The things I've seen going on after hours when I've been on my way home!" She waited for Emily to ask what she'd seen. Emily didn't like gossips and wasn't going to give her the satisfaction. But she wouldn't have been doing her job as a future crimes investigator if she didn't at least give a *tell me* tweak of her eyebrows. So that was what she did. The volunteer whispered, even though they were alone in the shop. "She gets dressed up."

"Isn't it a dressing-up shop?"

"She puts on wigs. Giant wigs. Like you'd see in a pantomime."

That was nothing! Most nights Emily couldn't get off the tube at Clapham Common and wait for the 137 bus to take her home to Brixton without seeing a least one person wearing a comedy wig. Wednesday night was cabaret night at the Two Brewers on Clapham

High Street. So was Thursday. So was Sunday. Actually, she was pretty sure Tuesday was cabaret night, too, come to think of it. But Emily didn't have time to stay and chat about comedy, cabaret, Clapham or wigs. She wanted to catch up with Hilary and Trina and find out why Hilary had reacted so defensively at the mention of drowning. She put the *Fawlty Towers* video back on the shelf, gave the volunteer a reassuring smile and left the shop.

Hilary and Trina were heading back up the hill in the direction of the hotel, with the town behind them and the sea to their left. It was no longer raining.

Emily fell into step with them. "Are you going back to the Majestic?"

"You staying there?" Trina pulled the sleeves down on her hoodie and shivered. "I bet it's nice inside."

"It is nice. Depends a bit which room you're staying in."

"Could I come and have a look?"

"We have work to do," said Hilary.

"Are you going out demonstrating? With the placards?" Emily was trying to be polite.

Trina looked down, kicking the toe of her shoe into the pavement as she walked. "Nah. She's got something else planned."

Hilary was brisk. "Look, it's perfectly safe, with the Colonel doing the immersing."

"Immersing?" said Emily. "You mean, putting something under water?"

"Come down to the beach with us," said Hilary. "See for yourself what it's all about."

"Why can't I be the one doing the immersing?" said Trina. "I'm strong. I could do it."

"You may have to," said Hilary. "If the Colonel packs up and leaves us."

This startled Trina. "Is he gonna?"

"You'd think Good Friday would give prime pickings if someone was out looking for souls to save. But people are only thinking of Easter eggs and Edmund Zenon."

"Did you know that woman in the shop?" asked Emily. "Madame Nova?"

Hilary ignored the question and spoke to Trina. "Hold fast to your family, whatever happens, whatever they may do. No matter how wickedly you think they've behaved."

"I can't. They've disowned me."

They were passing the last shop before the beach, a sweet shop called Sweet Harmony. A hand-painted sign of a Jersey cow with coquettish eyes swung gently above a window displaying toffee, fudge and coconut ice. The fudge was a sweet confection made locally from clotted cream and boiled sugar. The toffee was available in licorice, treacle and the standard caramelized sugar flavor. The pink-and-white-striped coconut ice was made from desiccated coconut and sugar boiled up and pressed into blocks. *That looks horrible*, thought Emily.

"That looks nice," said Hilary. "You've been ever so good since we got here, Trina. Do you want some toffee?"

"I need some new eyeliner."

"No, you don't. You wear too much as it is. You can have some toffee."

"I don't want toffee."

"Fudge, then. Coconut ice?"

Trina shrugged her shoulders. Hilary and Trina went into the shop. Emily followed them. Behind the counter there was a motherly woman in a pink-and-white-striped apron. Behind her, inevitably, was a poster showing Edmund Zenon walking on water.

"Those are everywhere!" said Emily, as Trina loaded the pocket of her hooded top with packets of fudge and coconut ice.

"Well, there was a lovely young man called Chris who came round to my shop yesterday. Told me something exciting was happening and I could be part of the magic."

"Yeah?" Trina was impressed.

"How can you refuse when it turns out he's only asking you to put up a poster!"

A lovely young man called Chris. So that was it. Madame Nova had known Chris's name because he had visited her shop and asked her to put up a poster. And when she had used his name as part of her fortune-telling routine and all the kids in the tea shop had got excited, Chris hadn't wanted to give away the "secret" about how it was done. Not even to Emily.

The motherly woman prattled on. "Immersive theater, he called it. I went home to my husband, Barney, and I said—"

Hilary cut her off. "Yes, well we've got our own bit of immersive theater to be getting on with. But ours isn't blasphemous. So good day to you." She left the shop.

Emily paused at the door to ask one final question of the woman behind the counter. "What did you think when you saw the poster?"

The woman smoothed her apron, tipped her chin up and smiled happily. "I thought: Finally! Something exciting's about to happen in this town, and it includes me. And it'll bring more customers to my shop."

◆　◆　◆

Hilary crossed the road and walked along the path above the beach, in the direction of the hotel, Trina and Emily following her. Looking down through the railings, Emily could see a small crowd on the beach watching what appeared to be some amateur sporting or athletic event. The tide was going out so there was a biggish expanse of wet sand to play on. But what were they playing? Was it a game of beach cricket? Was it a race?

As they drew closer, Emily decided it must be a race. One of the contestants was the preacher she had seen earlier, still in his white clothes, his trousers rolled up to his calves. He appeared to be pursuing the other contestant, who was wearing a tweedy jacket that flapped open as he ran, his arms flailing. The contestant being pursued was Gerald Ayode.

"Sir!" the preacher called. "Sir!"

Gerald wasn't an athletic man but he was going at a good pace.

The preacher's voice was hoarse. "Sir! Come into the waves with me!"

So it wasn't a race.

Gerald was a reformer. He was a zealous man. He had said as much yesterday. But when he had talked to Emily about the challenges of being the president of the Royal Society for the Exploration of Science and Culture, Emily never would have guessed one of those challenges would involve being called into the sea by a vigorous-looking preacher with his trousers at half-mast.

"Colonel!" called Hilary, dumping her plastic bags and running down the steps with Trina beside her. Her voice brought him to his senses. The preacher stopped chasing after Gerald and walked back to the enthralled crowd, who carefully remained out of arms' reach, taking a few steps backward as necessary, to protect themselves as he came near.

Gerald made it to the safety of the steps beneath where Emily was standing and he started climbing. The Colonel didn't even glance back in his direction. Like a fielder who has dropped his catch in a cricket match but must continue the game, he walked in his white trousers and white shirt to the edge of the field of play, head down, hands on hips, and started again.

So this was the Colonel who liked immersing people? It looked to Emily as if he hadn't had much luck this afternoon. His clothes were dry. Now he stood up to his ankles in the shallow waves and called out to the crowd, "Who will come into the water with me and be drowned, and emerge to be born again? Take the pledge; take the plunge!"

The Colonel was out of breath, gasping great raggedy breaths between words. But his melodious Welsh voice was still deep and powerful, carrying as far as Emily as she leaned against the railings above to listen.

Gerald came and stood next to Emily. He was also out of breath. He held onto the railings, concentrating on his out breaths as he calmed himself. "Maybe this is the drowning Peg's been seeing? A symbolic one. You can mention it in the report."

"I will."

Hilary and Trina had joined the crowd below. Emily saw that Tim was still among them. He must have been there for nearly an hour and a half listening to the Colonel preach.

Hilary grabbed the charity shop sundress and then she started shucking a complaining Trina out of her hoodie. But Trina wouldn't have it. So in the end Hilary put the dress over all of it—hooded top, jeans, sweater, all of it—and pushed her to the front.

The Colonel seemed surprised. He looked over at Hilary. "A volunteer?"

Hilary nodded.

"Are you sure now?" *Are you shoo-er now?* Two syllables. The Colonel's accent was very Welsh. It gave his voice a lovely lilting cadence that made everything he said seem like a prayer. "Are you sure, child?"

"I should have let him catch me," said Gerald. "Spared the girl. Should I go back down there?"

But Trina and the Colonel were already wading waist deep into the water. The waves were a little rough, but the Colonel was sure-footed. Emily was familiar enough with adult baptisms. She knew the way it was supposed to work. Trina would cross her arms over her chest and lay down in the crook of the Colonel's arm while he prayed over her. Then he would dip her down into the icy cold water while she lay motionless, not resisting, and then bring her up again, glowing from her immersion in the waves. It was a setup. But presumably Hilary had staged it so that, after seeing this, other people would want a turn. Or, if they didn't want to commit, they could at least go home and think on what they had seen and become closer to God.

With her report in mind, Emily turned over the implications of the staged salvation. If the Colonel wasn't having much luck getting people to come forward in the usual way, did that mean he was desperate, dangerous? He was desperate enough to chase Gerald down the beach. But would he be desperate enough to drown someone? And, even if he did, what might he hope to achieve by it?

In the sea, a few feet from the shore, Trina lay back in the crook of the Colonel's arm. Emily now realized that Hilary had chosen the dress for her to make her look girlish and pure of heart. But it quickly became heavy once the water got into it; it was at least two sizes too big. The hooded top was heavy, too, the waves filling the hood and pulling down on it.

The water was cold and quite deep. The Colonel was feeling it. Emily noticed he was shivering.

"I hope they don't go too far back," said Gerald. "It's quite rocky behind them, look."

A feisty little wave came in just as the Colonel was about to dip Trina down under the water. It unbalanced him slightly so that he dipped her a little further than was necessary. Trina gasped as she went under. She took in a mouthful of water. Her reflexes tried to bring her to the surface instead of letting her stay relaxed and lying in the crook of the Colonel's arm. But she couldn't come back up because her clothes were dragging her down, so she started struggling.

Another complication was that she had in the pocket of her hoodie packets of Devon fudge and pink-and-white-striped coconut ice, all of which would get heavy with water and drag down the material of the hoodie as if something like a fishhook had got caught in it.

Flinging her arms about, trying to get something to hold onto to bring her back to the surface, Trina accidentally punched the Colonel in the throat. He gasped and staggered back, and reflexively held Trina tighter, which seemed to frighten her.

"Do we need to do something?" asked Gerald. "What shall we do?"

Incongruously, Emily thought of Peg's positivity circle. Apart from beaming positive thoughts in Trina's direction, she couldn't think of anything useful to do. They were too far away to intervene. Besides, wasn't the Colonel used to immersing people? He must be used to this. It would be OK.

Trina tried to struggle free of him. He brought Trina up to the surface but staggered back again. He slipped on the rocks under his feet, going under. They were both struggling now. Trina was out of the Colonel's grip and tried to hurl herself toward the shore. But the current pulled her back. Trina was drowning. The Colonel reached for her, trying to grab her and steer her toward the beach.

Trina's non-waterproof Big Lash mascara and Nighttime Stay-on Smoky Accents eyeliner from Maybelline would be off her lids and lashes now and mixing with the salt seawater, stinging her eyes, making it difficult to see anything. She trod on the Colonel's shoulder as he reached for her, and she pushed him under, where his arms would be scraping on the sharp little rocks poking up from the sand on the seabed beneath them. He came up and Emily could see he was trying to get a hold of Trina. They went under again. They were drowning.

CHAPTER TEN
BORN AGAIN

Emily and Gerald ran down the steps. Emily, with a Londoner's ingrained reluctance to leave baggage unattended, had brought Hilary's plastic bags with her, banging against her legs as she ran.

They could see that Trina and the Colonel were in trouble, not "playing" or even worse "playing dolphins" as some people in the crowd would later claim to have believed. They were getting tired, they had been scratched as they were thrown against the sharp rocks under their feet, they had tried to reach the shore but they had been pulled back by the waves. They had gone under. If someone didn't do something, one or both of them would drown right in front of everyone, only feet from the shore.

Tim saw they were in trouble as well. As he had been standing among the crowd on the beach, he was only a few feet away from the drama. He ran into the water. He reached under the waves and got hold of Trina and hauled her to safety. With Trina out of the way, no longer kicking and flinging her arms about in panic, the Colonel recovered and stood up. He began to walk toward the beach, the cuts and scratches on his arms and face bleeding. Tim went back and took hold of the Colonel's arm and walked with him.

"Now, what are we supposed to make of that?" asked the Colonel. He was too shocked to say thank-you.

Hilary was at their side by now. She waved Emily over and took the two orange candlewick bedspreads out of the plastic bags. She threw one over Tim and the other over the Colonel. She put her own coat over Trina.

It seemed the Colonel now had the answer to his question. He turned his scratched, bleeding face to Tim. "*You* were the one who was meant to be immersed. That's what this is about. Consider yourself blessed and born again. What's your name, sir?"

"Tim."

"Let me buy you a drink up at the hotel, Tim."

Tim eyed the bedspreads and saw that Hilary had come prepared. "You knew this would happen?"

"Hardly!" said Hilary. "Not Trina trying to drown the Colonel and you saving them both. The two of them were supposed to have a quick dip and come out wet, that's all."

Trina was shivering violently, her mascara running down from her eyes in mock-zombie rivulets. "I'm going to die of cold."

"You can have a bath as soon as we get back to the Seaview," said Hilary. She rubbed Trina's arms as they walked along, to keep her circulation going. "That'll warm you up."

"The Hotel Majestic's just over the road," Tim said. "Trina can have a bath in my room." He was embarrassed. "I mean our room. Sarah, my wife . . ."

Trina rolled her zombie eyes. "We know what you meant."

"Thank you!" said Hilary. "That's kind of you. Saved again!"

"Thank you, Tim. Meet you there in a bit, Hilary," said the Colonel. "I'll go back to the Seaview and get changed."

"And can you bring Trina some dry clothes?" Hilary reminded him.

"I will. Tim, would you do me a favor? Could you let the security guards at the hotel know I'm meeting you?" Shivering, wet and bleeding, wearing an orange bedspread, he grinned. "Otherwise they might think I'm some sort of undesirable and not let me in."

CHAPTER ELEVEN

LIONS

Gerald used his position as president of the society and chair of the conference to clear a corner of the bar at the Hotel Majestic for the main players in the afternoon's drama, and their family and friends. Dr. Muriel, Peg and Sarah Taylor squashed together on a sofa with Emily and Gerald, Sarah sitting next to Peg, her new best friend. Hilary perched on a bar stool slightly apart from the group, with Tim's discarded sodden bedspread rolled up in a plastic bag at her feet, waiting while Trina had a bath upstairs in Tim and Sarah's room.

Gerald fiddled with his phone. "I'm checking Twitter now. I can't see any photos of the debacle on the beach," he said to Emily. "Not under the hashtag BeliefandBeyond, anyway. So that's a relief."

Tim came in and stood at the bar, waiting to catch the barman's eye to get himself a drink. His hair was damp and he was wearing several layers of clothes, but otherwise he seemed unaffected by his plunge into the sea. He responded to polite enquiries from the group about his welfare by explaining he had used the hot shower in the hotel spa to clean up and warm up and he was now perfectly OK.

Trina wafted in wearing a big pair of trousers and a flowery top that Sarah had lent her. She smelled of a mix of several of the finest products supplied by the perfumeries of Grasse, and she had a shiny face.

Sarah smiled. "Been at my face creams, Trina?"

"Yeah. Well they're no use to you. You've already lost your looks."

95

Sarah flushed.

Hilary turned on Trina. "That's enough of your lip!"

"It's OK," said Sarah. Her expressive eyebrow-raise/shoulder-raise combo gesture said, *Teenagers!* And everybody who saw it knew she'd rather have her son there being rude to her than dead and gone, and they were sorry for her loss.

Fortunately Peg was in good spirits. She turned the conversation away from troublesome or absent teenagers and back to her favorite subject: herself. "We need to send out a press release, Gerald. Lady Lacey Carmichael must be celebrating today's news, wherever she is. Eh? What do you reckon, Emily? You must be celebrating and all, dear. You write up that report and you can take the rest of the weekend off."

Gerald looked anxious. Hadn't he suffered enough for one day after being chased down the beach by the Colonel? "I don't think we can say it's proved, Peg. I really don't."

"I saw a man drowning in my vision."

"You knew the Colonel was going to drown?" Hilary shifted her bar stool a little closer.

"Not the Colonel, no. I wasn't able to pinpoint the identity of the victim. As a matter of fact, we thought it might be Edmund. But I saw a man drowning—choking, going under the waves. I brought together my circle of like-minded women, all strong and free spirited, and we sent out good vibes to save him. And save him we did. Prophesy plus positivity equals success! Sales of my book are going to go through the roof."

"Perhaps it was a coincidence?" said Gerald.

"Well, I'm surprised at you, since you're supposed to be the science-minded one here, Gerald. But Muriel will back me up, I'm sure. There's no such thing as coincidence."

Dr. Muriel shifted her arm to try to get more comfortable. "We all have different ways of interpreting events, that's what's so interesting about it. I'm doing a talk at the conference tomorrow about mythmaking. I do hope you'll be able to join me."

But Peg wasn't going to be cheated of her moment in the spotlight. "I'll put another call in to the features editor of the *Sunday Sentinel*, see if she can't do something about the important work that's been done here. It's not a myth. Or coincidence. It's what I like to call cosmic influence."

Hilary was unimpressed. "It's what *I* like to call cosmic nonsense!"

"Call it what you like, dear. But good luck pitching a feature to the Sunday papers on cosmic nonsense."

Joseph Seppardi came into the bar and cooled the atmosphere by a few degrees, like a robot that has been designed to look like a man but behaves like a portable air conditioner. He saw that Sarah was sitting with Peg but he made no move to join them. He stood awkwardly by the bar. "Sarah," he said. "What time should we get together this evening?"

"I think we should leave it for this evening, Joe. Thanks."

This wasn't the answer he was expecting. He stood there waiting for an explanation.

"I've got some bits to do. Might get an early night. Me and Tim are going on the Agatha Christie tour tomorrow, and you've got a big day, haven't you?"

"Sarah—"

"*We're* still on for six o'clock, though, dear?" Peg said to Sarah.

Sarah barely glanced at Joseph as she said, "Maybe we shouldn't."

"Don't let *him* dictate what you can do," said Peg.

Sarah blundered on anxiously, trying to smother any sparks of rage in Joseph with words, lots of words, a blanket of words. "It's on a vintage bus. The trip to Agatha Christie's house. I'd like Tim to see it. Take his mind off . . . off of . . . Take his mind off . . ."

"His immersion?" enquired Joseph.

"Well, no. I think he quite enjoyed that, in a funny sort of way. He's come out of it feeling more positive than when he went in."

"Has he indeed?" said Joseph. "Then what does he need to take his mind off? Not his son?"

Sarah looked at him, mute with misery, one side of her face turning red as though she'd been slapped.

The Colonel turned up just then, oblivious to the tension in the room. He greeted Hilary by saying, as if he had made some extraordinarily useful contribution to their domestic arrangements, "I've put that bedspread in the bathroom to dry, Hilary."

He handed over clean clothes to Trina and went over to Gerald.

"I owe you an apology," he said. "Can I make a donation, perhaps, to a favorite charity?

"No need," said Gerald graciously.

"I chased you down on the sand, sir—"

"Gerald."

"I chased you down on the sand, Gerald, and made you look a fool."

Gerald looked uncomfortable at that. No man wants to be reminded that he has recently been made to look foolish.

"I was feeling very low," the Colonel said. "Desperate. I stood on the sand and I called for people to take a plunge in the water with me, and no one responded. At that moment, I had lost my faith."

"Ah. Well. No harm done. You got there in the end."

"And then I saw you, and my mind turned to Africa, you see. I had been thinking of taking a trip there, before too long."

Trina looked at Hilary. Hilary sat stone-faced on her bar stool.

The Colonel carried on, still oblivious. "I saw a black man in front of me and I thought . . . Oh, excuse me. Where are *you* from, Gerald?"

"Ealing. West London." Gerald tried to put his left hand out to indicate the westness of it, so the Colonel could bring to mind a map of London and locate Ealing on it, but there wasn't much room. He had to keep his elbow tucked in. "It's on the District Line—the green one."

"Well, I saw a black man in front of me and I lost my head. I thought of Africa."

"That's racist!" said Trina.

"No, it isn't," said Hilary.

"Yes it is."

"No, it isn't."

"I don't mind," said Gerald. "I'm proud of my race. I'm proud to be the first black president of the Royal Society for the Exploration of Science and Culture." He looked over at Emily as if to say, *you can write that down.* She took out her notebook.

The Colonel continued. "I saw you and I thought of Africa. I thought of lions. I thought of all the souls I could save if I left Britain and went there. I believed it was a sign. I was meant to immerse you."

Hilary chipped in, trying to keep her voice calm. "There are lions in Trafalgar Square. Two big pools with fountains. Think of all the people you could immerse in there."

The Colonel looked sad. "We've never had much luck in London, have we?"

Now Trina piped up again. "You found *me*!"

The Colonel spoke gently to her. "Yes, child. So we did. But you'll be back in school soon enough, won't you?"

"What do you mean? I ain't been in school since I was ten!"

Squished together, Peg and Sarah looked at each other and made silent *awww* faces that could be seen by everybody in their corner of the bar except the Colonel, who was looking at Trina.

"Hilary will find a place for you, child. The Easter holiday will be over soon. You can't neglect your education."

"I'm not a child!" Trina yelled, loud enough for a philosopher from Manchester and a philosopher from Stockholm to stop talking and look over at her, even though they were sitting all the way at the other side of the bar. Other delegates in the bar looked over, too. They saw a child dressed in a middle-aged woman's clothing, standing in a hotel bar, asserting loudly that she was not a child. Then they noticed Dr. Muriel and . . . well, to the philosophy professors, at least, nothing seems out of place when you put another philosophy professor into the mix. They must have hypothesized that this was a practice for the illustration of some ethical conundrum at Dr. Muriel's talk at the conference on Sunday morning. The philosophers nodded and smiled and waved. Everybody went back to their drinks. The buzz of conversation resumed in the bar.

"And Tim!" said the Colonel, going to stand next to him. "I said I'd buy you a drink, my friend. But that hardly seems enough, considering what you have done for me. How much is that magician fella offering this weekend?"

"Fifty thousand pounds," said Tim.

"I was full of doubts. I stood by the waves and called for people to come in. But you were the only one who responded. So I'll match the magician's fifty thousand pounds."

"You what?" said Trina.

"I'd like to make a donation of fifty thousand pounds to a charity of your choice, Tim. Never mind the paranormal. You have proved something much more important to me."

"Now, hang on a moment," Hilary said.

"You've got fifty thousand pounds?" Trina said. "And we've been stuck in that Seaview place that smells of sick and mold?"

"We don't need money," said the Colonel. "It's not important, the life we lead. Think how much further the funds would go in Africa—the souls we could save."

"We could be staying here," said Trina. "You know there's a spa? With a Jacuzzi!"

"I'll get us a room here if it means that much to you, child."

"I think they're fully booked," said Hilary.

Tim caught hold of the Colonel's elbow, very lightly, and brought the subject back to the Colonel's money. "You were talking about making a charitable donation?"

Joseph Seppardi put his drink down loudly enough to attract attention from their group. As all eyes in the corner of the room turned to him, he closed his and began to breathe deeply, hands clasped in front of his chin.

"What is it, Joe?" Sarah asked anxiously.

But Joseph Seppardi didn't last even a minute as the center of attention. Two attractive men—one dark haired, one blond—walked through the bar, turning heads. The atmosphere crackled with excitement.

"You're not prancing about doing street mime *now* for a few coins in a hat!" the dark-haired one was saying, good-naturedly enough. "This isn't some earnest government-funded poetry event with acrobats and out-of-work actors in masks."

"Good to hear it. Those kinds of events take a hell of a lot of work."

They could have been brothers, or two men playing brothers in a popular soap opera: both arrogant and athletic looking, one dark, one blond, quarreling over their opposing world views, yet comfortable in each other's company. It was Edmund Zenon and Chris, and they were heading in Emily's direction.

"I believe I have something of yours," Edmund said. With a magician's flourish, he produced a key, apparently out of the air. He held it out to Emily and bowed theatrically, as if he was presenting her with a bunch of flowers. "Room number thirty-six. I'll get my luggage collected this evening. Please accept the key with my apologies."

"Is that the big room at the front? The one with the balcony?" Peg asked, a little jealously.

"It isn't mine," Emily told her. "It was meant for Dr. Muriel. There was a mix-up at check-in."

"What a lovely gesture, Edmund," said Dr. Muriel. "I truly appreciate it. But I'm settled in upstairs now. All my clothes unpacked and various electricals charging. I shan't change rooms with you. You keep it."

"There's a room free?" Trina looked very excited. "Hilary?"

"Out of the question!" snarled Hilary.

Trina snatched the bag of clothes the Colonel had brought and hugged it to herself, brooding, as if the bag contained an elaborate costume that would transform her into her alter ego, a terrifying comic book villain.

The attention of the group in the corner of the bar turned back to itself.

Tim said to Joseph Seppardi, "Was it Liam? Just now? What was he saying?"

Joseph Seppardi shook his head. "He's gone."

"You should be ashamed of yourself," Edmund said to Joseph. "Preying on vulnerable people. You charlatan."

"*You* should be ashamed," said Sarah. "He helps people like us. He gives us hope. What do you do?"

"Save your soul, Edmund," said Hilary. "Before it's too late. The Colonel can do it for you."

"Pledge and plunge?" said Edmund. "No thanks. If I'm going to make a show of myself in public, I like to get paid for it."

"It doesn't have to be public," said the Colonel. "Make your peace with God. Go into the water, Edmund. No one needs to know except the One Above."

"What if he ain't got a soul to save?" Trina was genuinely interested. "Who'll help him then?"

"Ah," said Gerald. "Now, here we all are, gathered for a conference that we hope will give rise to some interesting discussion about what people believe and why. Let's try to keep things civil."

"I'll drink to that." Dr. Muriel raised her glass. "Why don't you tell us about your challenge, Edmund?"

It was Gerald who answered her. "We've got the security guards in place. That's the most important thing."

"To protect Edmund?"

Edmund laughed. "To stop the contestants coming out of the Ballroom tomorrow and telling everyone else the secret method we used to evaluate their skills."

Gerald exchanged a conspiratorial look with Edmund. He was obviously in on the secret—and wanted people to know it.

Sarah looked worried. "What secret method? I thought you'd just say, you know, 'Give me your best shot.'"

Joseph Seppardi said, "I shan't be taking part in it, Sarah."

"I'm sure it'll be fascinating!" said Dr. Muriel. "I wish I could see it."

Edmund treated her to his charismatic smile. "Can you keep a secret?"

"If it's interesting enough to make it worth my while!"

Were Edmund and Dr. Muriel *flirting* with each other? Emily exchanged a horrified look with Trina, the only other youngish person in their group. Trina raised her eyebrows. No one else seemed to mind.

Edmund twirled the key in his fingers. "Why don't you drop into the Ballroom tomorrow, then, Muriel? I owe you a favor, for being so gracious about the mix-up with the room."

"Oh yes! And Emily, too. She's marvelous with secrets."

"And me!" said Trina. "Can I come?"

Edmund gave her a nice smile. "I can't allow bystanders, Trina. I'm sorry. We've got all sorts of nondisclosure and other legal forms."

"Emily's part of the team, so she'll be OK," said Dr. Muriel. "She's our future crimes unit."

"What does that involve?" Edmund looked amused.

"She's writing a report about my premonition, and how I saved the Colonel from drowning," Peg told him.

Chris turned to Emily. "So you're not on holiday, then?" He looked hurt. "That's why you were taking such an interest when we were in the Rosie? You're here to write about Edmund?"

"Dinnertime, I think!" said Gerald. "Muriel? Emily? Peg? You're joining me, is that right?"

As the members of their group edged up from the sofa and trod on each other's feet and reached across each other for jackets and cardigans hung over the back of their seats, Chris walked off. Emily called after him. If he heard her, he didn't acknowledge it. It would have been absurd to go chasing after him, so she stayed and watched him walk away.

"We need to talk through the day's events," said Gerald. "Do you fancy a pie and a pint at the Lamb and Dragon? They're doing a special offer this weekend." His invitation took in Peg, Dr. Muriel and Emily.

"Why don't you try the Poisson d'Avril, by the pier?" Edmund said. "It's a nice place, if a little overpriced."

"Ah, well. The budget . . ."

"Book a table at the Poisson d'Avril, Gerald. Make sure you ask for one near the window. You won't regret it."

"Nice view?"

"There should be, tonight."

Chapter Twelve
Walking on Water

Later, people would talk about where they were and what they were doing when it happened, though no one could agree who had seen it first. They were on the big wheel overlooking the harbor. They were eating fish and chips by the pier. They were walking the dog. They were smoking a cigarette outside the pub. They were going home from work. They were going out to get drunk.

The sky was dark because the sun had set, but there were only a few clouds drifting across the full moon as it climbed in the sky, dripping silvery beauty over everything below it. The night air was chilly but pleasant. Though it was out of season, there were plenty of people about because they were either attending the Belief and Beyond conference, or enjoying the fringe activities that went with it. Colored lights had been strung along the esplanade and looped around the palm trees. The sea was calm. If not quite the Riviera, Torquay nevertheless seemed magical and charming as Emily took her seat by the window in the Poisson d'Avril restaurant on the top floor of a three-story building next to the pier, overlooking the harbor.

Emily, Dr. Muriel, Peg and Gerald had ordered fish and chips with a bottle of the house white wine. Gerald had taken a picture of the food when it arrived, to put it on Twitter: *Good Friday fish supper #BeliefandBeyond.*

"How's the report going?" Gerald asked Emily.

"The image of Edmund walking on water is where it starts for me. I mean, seeing the poster was where the story started to get real—looking at him, seeing his face, his eyes. I felt a connection to him. That image seems to suggest different things to different people. Some think it's blasphemous. Some think it's about entertainment, or money. Some think they're looking at a man who will drown. It's like . . ."

Dr. Muriel said, "It's like a spiritualist or a psychic whose real skill is showing people to themselves. They use a mirror, not a microscope." She smiled at Peg. "Or so the studies say, anyway."

"I'll agree with you there, Muriel," said Peg. "There are those of us who have the gift, of course. But I'm afraid there's also charlatans. You take that Joseph Seppardi, for one. You seen the way he manipulates that poor couple, Sarah and Tim? He'll say he's talking to their child, but he's just telling Sarah what she wants to hear. He doesn't have the kind of skills to bring to a situation and turn it around the way I can with my positivity circle. You've got all that in your report, Emily? A drowning foretold, and it's all over and done with, fortunately, with the Colonel surviving the ordeal."

"Yes. But I thought it was Edmund who was going to drown," said Emily.

"You're a sensitive and intelligent person, but your aura still needs development. Remind me to give you some lessons when we get back to London," Peg snapped.

"Sounds like the report's shaping up nicely," said Gerald, very quick. "It'll show the excitement we've generated in Torquay by bringing the conference to town, and how it can have a positive impact on the tourist trade in other locations, if we decide to spread our wings." He changed the subject. "That haddock looks good, Peg. How is it?"

"Very nice. But you should have been a bit quicker if you wanted a picture for your Twit-thing, Gerald. It's nearly all gone."

"I'm glad you enjoyed it," said Gerald smoothly. "The cod in batter's good. A bit bland, perhaps. But it was the most reasonably priced choice on the menu."

"Haddock's reliable. I don't like to get the cod because of over-fishing," said Peg. It was the last mundane thing anyone would say for a while because people had already started to run toward the window, calling excitedly to each other that the magician, in top hat and black cape, had begun to walk along a stone jetty by the pier.

Emily and her companions put down their wine glasses and went to the window to watch. The moon was full but it was dark outside. Powerful lights had been strung up at the town end of the jetty to pick out the figure of the magician, and these were switched on as soon as he began to walk toward the sea. The lights were housed in a specially constructed temporary booth made from scaffolding, with a waterproof canvas above it to protect the lights in case of rain. One of the security guards from the hotel was standing by the booth to make sure no one got too close.

The magician was going to do a trick. And everyone knew what he was going to do because it had been staring them in the face all day, and they had been expecting it, even if they hadn't *known* they were expecting it. He was going to walk on water. From their position by the window in the Poisson d'Avril restaurant, Emily and the other three had a good view of the show. There was Edmund in top hat and cape, walking *very* slowly along the jetty, putting one foot in front of the other as though he were walking on a tightrope, building the tension, allowing time for the crowd to grow bigger, the excitement to increase.

Gerald had his phone out and was spelling a message on it with his thumb. *Big crowd here! #BeliefandBeyond*

Down below them, Emily could see people running toward the jetty from all directions, trying to find a position that would give them a good view. A couple of youths had climbed the lampposts. Some men had children or girlfriends on their shoulders, as if they were at a festival in a park. There were coin-operated telescopes along the esplanade but these were fixed in place, pointing at places of interest across the bay, and money put into them tonight would be wasted unless the viewer wanted to look at those places and hear an accompanying recorded commentary. Most people had gone down onto the beach. Emily thought she spotted some familiar faces among them. There was Tim—tall and therefore easily identifiable among the crowd—a rucksack over his shoulder, zigzagging through the crowd. And then, twenty paces behind, as if tailing him, there was the slightly taller Joseph Seppardi. There were the German professors, Marta and Birgitte, and others from the conference whose names and nationalities Emily had forgotten or didn't yet know. There was Hilary, too, though she was walking away from the crowd, heading into town.

Edmund was nearly at the end of the jetty, all eyes on him, when there was the sound of furious shouting.

It was the Colonel, wading into the water from the beach in his white shirt with his trousers rolled up, his jacket discarded on the shore. He called to the magician from the waves. "Blasphemer!"

The lights that had been trained on Edmund flickered. The crowd lost sight of him for a moment or two. Where was he? Who would see him first and have the satisfaction of shouting it for others to hear? A lad up a lamppost saw him, shouting like the kid on the *Titanic* who has seen the iceberg. *There he is! There!* It was impressive. He really did look as though he was walking on the water. He proceeded slowly, arms out for balance, still putting his feet heel to toe, one in front of the other, like a tightrope walker.

"Oh! Now that's a good trick," said Dr. Muriel.

"Is the Colonel part of it, do you think?" asked Gerald, a little anxiously.

"Aren't you in on this?" Dr. Muriel asked him.

"No. I've been involved with the paranormal challenge, to ensure it's as rigorous as possible and conducted along broadly scientific lines. But this trick is something Edmund's taken upon himself to do. I hope the Colonel doesn't do anything silly."

Emily looked along the jetty to see if she could see Chris. He would be at the heart of it somewhere. She couldn't see him anywhere among the huge crowd. "I don't think the Colonel's part of the show."

"Someone's going to call the police if they think he's threatening Edmund," said Gerald. "I need to go down there." He tweaked at the sleeves of his jacket and adjusted his necktie with as much resolve as any action hero. But he remained by the window.

Emily wasn't surprised at Gerald's reluctance to approach the Colonel at the water's edge, given the afternoon's events. She said, "I'll go down there. I'll see if I can persuade the Colonel to come back out of the sea."

When she reached the jetty, pushing her way through the crowds, Emily could hear the Colonel railing at the magician in a language she didn't recognize.

"Chware'n troi'n chwerw." He was chest-deep in the water in his white shirt. *"Dros ben llestri!"*

The crowd that had gathered on the beach didn't seem to recognize the language either.

"He's speaking in tongues!"

"It's Arabic!"

"It's Hebrew!"

"Black magic!"

"It's a curse! He's putting a curse on the magician! He wants him to drown!"

Emily looked out to sea but she couldn't see Edmund.

"He's gone under!" someone shouted.

"The preacher's put a curse on him!"

"He's drowning!"

"He's disappeared!"

"Call the coastguard! Dial 999!"

All around her, Emily could hear people shouting into their mobile phones, the screens lighting up like candles at a vigil as they called the emergency services, or called their friends and reported that Edmund Zenon had vanished. And they'd been there to see it! They took pictures of the darkness so they could show their friends later. *This is where he disappeared. This empty bit here is where he should have been.*

There were lifebelts positioned every few feet along the railings. Someone unhooked one and threw it into the sea, where it bobbed unhelpfully a few feet from shore. Someone else followed suit. Soon the sea was littered with lifebelts, floating on the water like floral tributes.

As Emily looked in vain for a sign of Edmund, she could hear people all around her, discussing what they had seen.

"What happened?" she asked some of the young lads standing near her.

The explanations came tumbling out, not all of them helpful.

"So, he's walking along the jetty, then the lights blink and then there he is, walking on water!"

"My mate Jimmy saw something was going on and he texted me and we all ran down here."

"His cape billowing. Like a sail. Big and black, with a slash of red."

"Like a pirate's sail!"

"I reckon he was, like, on a skateboard. A Perspex skateboard."

"Or he had something strapped on his feet, like snowshoes, but for the water."

"Or a surfboard?"

"It doesn't matter what he had. It didn't work. *He's drowned!*"

Emily left them and walked closer to the pier, trying to make sense of what had happened. If Edmund had drowned, then how could Peg and the other psychics possibly have predicted it? Things like that never happened. Unless somebody had been inspired by the predictions to sabotage the trick. Unless . . . Where was Chris?

A woman of about Emily's age, in a short dress and a veil with a tiara, was staggering around by the pier like a shell-shocked Marine. She was drunk. She was accompanied by a plump young woman in a pale blue satin spaghetti-strap dress and a fake tiara, carrying a quilted, sequined clutch bag, no coat.

"Did you see what happened?" Emily asked them.

The woman in the veil answered. "I was in the VIP booth of the big wheel with my bridesmaid, Chantal. It's my hen night."

"It was a *nightmare* when me and Jackie realized what was happening," Chantal said. She was also drunk. "We wanted to see and we couldn't get down there! We had to sit tight in that booth, going up higher and higher."

"Away from the action!" Jackie's voice was hoarse from shouting. "We were being pulled away from the action!"

"We was *desperate*," said Chantal. "We shouted for them to stop the ride."

"And they did!" said Jackie proudly.

Emily had her notebook out. "So what did you see? You saw his cape? His top hat?"

"I seen him go under," Jackie said. "I seen him drown."

Emily suspected it wasn't true—she had just said she was being pulled away from the action. But this was her big night, after all.

Chantal was also proud of their part in the story. "We knew what was gonna happen, anyway. Madame Nova seen it in Jackie's palm."

There was a young couple in the crowd who Emily recognized but couldn't place. He was wearing a knitted hat. She was slim and ghostlike beside him. Ben and Alice! From the train.

Ben saw Emily's notebook and came over, pulling Alice with him by the hand. He wanted to have his say. "Oh man! Did you see it? We were standing right there." He pointed to a spot close to the pier. "The lights blinked and we lost sight of him, and then he was walking on the water, very slow, heading out to sea."

Emily closed her notebook and put it back in her bag. "Was there anyone else down there? Another man? With blond hair."

"Just the magician."

"People are saying he's drowned."

Alice said, "It's a trick, Emily. For Easter. He's pretending to be dead and he'll rise again. It was *amazing*. And he's done it for free."

Emily wasn't sure. Where was he? And where was Chris?

Ben grabbed hold of Alice's hand, ready to go back to the action. "But that wasn't even the interesting part, really."

"What was, then?"

"That man, like King Neptune, raging and shouting in the water."

"I don't think he's part of it."

"He should be."

The Colonel. He was still chest-deep in the water, still shouting. If she couldn't locate Edmund or Chris, at least she could try to bring him in, as she had promised Gerald she would. But how? She went and stood on the beach as close to where he was standing as she could get, and she yelled at him. "Colonel!" But her voice wasn't as powerful as his. And anyway he was making such a commotion, she was pretty sure he wouldn't be able to hear her. *"Colonel!"* She would have to take off her shoes and socks and wade into the sea if she wanted to get close enough to talk any sense into him.

Fortunately she was saved from having to do this because Tim ran past her, dumped his rucksack by the end of the jetty and hurled himself into the sea to save the Colonel for the second time that day. Unattended baggage! Emily went and guarded Tim's rucksack. She couldn't help herself, honestly.

There was applause from several onlookers on the beach when they saw Tim run into the water. They were keen for any kind of entertainment until the coastguards turned up with boats and helicopters and started searching the water for Edmund Zenon. Where were they?

But the Colonel didn't want to come back to shore. He was still turned in the direction of the spot where Edmund had disappeared. "Blasphemer!" At least he was speaking English now, so the people on the shore could follow along. He tried to pull away from Tim to go deeper into the water. It was cold, it was dark and he was exhausted. If he wasn't careful, he was going to drown.

Tim started singing, a little reedily but perfectly in tune. *"Dear Lord and Father of mankind, forgive our foolish ways! Reclothe us in our rightful mind—"*

The hymn seemed to calm the Colonel and bring him back to his "rightful mind." He stopped struggling and responded in his deep, Welsh voice with the final words from the hymn. *"Let sense be dumb, let flesh retire; Speak through the earthquake, wind and fire, O still, small voice of calm."* He allowed Tim to begin leading him back through the water toward the shore.

But now, throwing himself into the water just as determinedly as Tim, but with more of a splash, here was Joseph Seppardi. He reached for Tim, who was still holding onto the Colonel. If he was attempting a rescue, he made a poor job of it. All three men went down and began thrashing around like sharks beaching themselves in shallow water.

Now Emily could just about make out yet another figure wading through the water, breathing heavily. He was going against the traffic, wading back to shore, barely visible until he was almost in front of her because of the dark diving suit he was wearing. He pulled down the hood and rubbed his hand through his hair. It was Chris. His teeth were chattering.

Emily picked up the rucksack and met him at the edge of the water. "Are you all right? What's happened?"

"It's all right, Emily. I'm all right."

"Where's Edmund? Should I go in? Should I try and look for him?"

Chris stood bent over, palms on his thighs, gasping.

"Chris, where's the magician?"

"He's gone."

Somewhere nearby, a woman started shrieking.

Chapter Thirteen

How to Disappear

"There!" she shrieked. "Up there!"

Others joined in, pointing, shouting. Cameras and phones flashed ineffectually. People clapped their hands, whooped and wolf whistled. They wanted to show their appreciation—and they wanted the people around them to know they had seen what they were meant to see. It wasn't too long until everyone faced in the same direction, looking up.

There, in the picture window of the Poisson d'Avril restaurant, framed against the warm yellow of the light in the room, like a Victorian silhouette portrait of a traditional stage magician: Edmund Zenon. His black top hat and his cape ensured he was easily recognizable to those too far away to make out his features. He turned to his right and bowed. He turned to his left and bowed. He turned full on to the crowd and bowed. That wasn't enough for them. They were still shrieking and waving. So he waved his hand and bowed again. Then he stepped back from the window out of sight, show over.

So Edmund Zenon hadn't drowned. Of course he hadn't. How could she have believed he would? Emily turned to Chris, who was standing straight and breathing normally, but still shivering. He took the rucksack from her and put it by his feet. Then he stripped off the diving suit and stood in the long johns he was wearing underneath, pulled warm clothes out of the bag—his clothes—and put them on.

Chris looked over at the mantangle of the Colonel, Tim and Joseph Seppardi, now emerging dripping wet from the sea, like some monstrous three-headed mutation of Colin Firth's Mr. Darcy emerging from the pond at Pemberley. "I'm going back to the hotel. I'll walk back with these guys."

"Was the Colonel part of the trick?"

"No. He was trying to ruin it. The ultimate heckle! You try to plan for every possibility so you'll know how to deal with it: bad weather, drunk people, lack of interest. But a renegade gate-crashing preacher wasn't on my list. Never mind."

"What about Tim?"

Chris grinned. "No, I asked him to bring my bag down, that's all. People don't mind helping, if you ask them. It went well, you think? Good crowd."

"Yes. Very appreciative. Look, Chris, I better get back to the restaurant."

"Got your report to write?" From the expression on his face, it was obvious he wanted Emily to say that she didn't care about the report or Edmund, she cared about him.

She said, "My dinner'll be getting cold."

◆　◆　◆

To get back to the restaurant, Emily had to fight her way past several excitable young women wearing fairy wings, waving light-up wands and half-empty bottles of Prosecco. The remainder of Jackie's hen party, presumably. The women were shrieking and laughing, but most of the rest of the people on the beach were milling about in the dark, not sure what to do with themselves, like disappointed guests at a poorly organized barbecue.

The entrance to the stairs leading up to the Poisson d'Avril was now guarded by Derek, one of the security guards from the hotel. Derek recognized Emily and stood aside so she could run up the three flights to rejoin her friends. They were sitting at their table by the window with Edmund Zenon. The bottle of house wine had been upgraded to a celebratory Pouilly Fumé.

Edmund was still in his stage costume: dinner jacket, cape and top hat. One thing seemed strange to Emily. His clothes were dry. He raised his glass to his companions at the table, smiling. "You enjoyed the show?"

"It was a very good trick," said Gerald. "Very good indeed. May I? This'll reassure people." He held up his phone and took a picture of Edmund. *The magician reappears! #BeliefandBeyond*

Edmund said, "I'm sorry if people were frightened—it wasn't my intention. I'm an entertainer, not a ghoul. The walking on water, the vanishing, the reappearing . . . It was supposed to be a marvelous spectacle, not something to frighten people."

"What about the coastguards?" Emily said. "The police? People started calling as soon as you disappeared."

"Good question, Emily." He spoke as if she were a bright pupil, not a grown woman. "I talked to the police commissioner before I came down here, to clear everything. They brought in extra staff at the call center, briefed them to ignore any calls about a drowning magician, and I paid the overtime. I'll also make a donation to the coastguards. Brave men and women. Where would we be without them?"

"You're a clever one," said Peg.

Edmund accepted a top-up of wine. "Isn't anyone going to try and guess how I did it?"

There was a polite silence.

Edmund laughed good-naturedly. "There's a lot of complex planning for something that seems artless. I suppose I just want to show off about it. I'm proud of my team."

Whatever Chris had done for his part in the trick, gasping for breath in his diving suit by the jetty, it had obviously been hard work. And he'd hinted that he'd also been involved in the planning. If taking a guess would be considered praise for the team, then Emily was prepared to play along. "I think you must have used a projector for the walking on water bit. Those lights shining down the jetty, they weren't just illuminating your image. Once you stepped from the jetty onto the sea, they were creating it. I don't know how it works exactly, but it's a bit like going through a tunnel on a train, and you see another version of yourself outside the window."

"Yes, you're right, Emily. Don't go putting it on Twitter, Gerald. It's an old Victorian stage illusion, called a Pepper's Ghost. We used projectors. But that wasn't the half of it. That's the technical part, which is concerned with what people see. We also had to do a bit of work beforehand, a bit of mental massaging to help the spectators with what they *think* they'll see. Here's a question for you: What's the best way of discovering something interesting?"

Emily didn't like being treated like the star pupil at a take-your-magician-to-work day, and she had no idea what answer he expected from her, but she gave her best answer anyway. "Go to a library?"

"Word of mouth. A buzz. Your friend tells you to come quickly, there's something amazing just over there. Or a stranger in the street starts running, and then someone else joins in and you follow, to see what's happened. We're programmed to react to natural phenomena— a beautiful sunset, a rainbow, a shooting star—by discovering, reacting and sharing. We wanted people to feel they had stumbled on the trick themselves. Discovering it adds another layer of enjoyment. So rather than advertising a start time, we seeded bits of information around town by word of mouth. Teenagers, shop owners, old men in the pubs. We hinted that something was going to happen, but we didn't say what."

"You did it pretty well," said Emily. "All the people talking about drowning. Was that part of it?"

"No! Nearly derailed my trick, actually. People were supposed to see a man who walks on water and then disappears and then . . . *pfft!* He reappears again, in a completely different place. That was the magic. *How did he do that? How did he get up there?* That was supposed to be the reaction. Instead, they saw a drowning man. Phones out. Coastguards called. Thankfully I was paying overtime." He sighed. "Well, that's just how it goes with a trick like this. Chris calls it immersive theater—everyone's part of the performance, even the unscripted people. That's what makes it exciting, I guess. OK, before the mob tries to storm its way up here to congratulate me, I had better disappear again."

"How're you going to do that?" said Peg. "There's only one way down."

"They're looking for a man in a cape and a top hat. If I remove those . . ."

He removed his top hat. He removed his cape. Now he was just a handsome man in ordinary clothes, not "the magician."

Peg nodded. "That's clever. Simple but clever. I'll give you that."

"Would you mind?" said Edmund to Emily, of his discarded pile of props. "I need someone to bring them back to the hotel."

She did mind, actually. But she accepted a bag with the neatly folded cape and the hat in it when he handed it to her.

"Shall we call it a night?" said Gerald, as they watched Edmund walk out of the restaurant. "At least we can rest easy in our beds knowing that—despite two near misses—no one has drowned today."

"So that just leaves tomorrow," said Dr. Muriel. "And Sunday."

"It's not gonna happen," said Peg. "It's over. I told you."

"I don't know," said Emily. "Someone's gone to a lot of trouble 'seeding information' about a drowning. Everyone's been talking about it."

"You're not accusing me, dear?" asked Peg.

"No. But someone has been setting the stage here in Torquay as carefully as Edmund."

"*Who?*" Gerald and Peg and Dr. Muriel asked, all together.

"Madame Nova."

"Eh?"

"Pardon?"

"Who?"

"A local fortune-teller. She's been popping up all over the place, talking about drowning. I bet if you check your emails, Peg, you'll find she was one of the first to contact you after Edmund's posters went up in Torquay. But I don't know why. Edmund's trick and the premonition about the drowning are two separate things. Whatever's gonna happen, it's still gonna happen. I'm not saying someone will drown, but this story hasn't played out to the end yet."

"We just need to keep this Madame Nova out of the hotel, that's all," said Gerald. "I'll talk to security. It'll be OK."

But it wasn't.

CHAPTER FOURTEEN
A GHOST? A WERECREATURE?

Gerald rang the bell for the night porter when they got back to the Hotel Majestic. As he left the reception desk and headed to the glass door to unlock it, they looked for their delegates' passes for him to inspect on their way in.

"It's here somewhere, I know it is," said Peg, rummaging through her handbag. "What a bother, all this security. It's a wonder you didn't ask for a full-body scanner at the door, Gerald. And pity the poor people who haven't got delegates' passes. Do they sleep on the streets?"

"They show their room keys," Emily said, holding up hers.

Gerald ignored Peg and spoke to the night porter. "I wonder if you'd do me a favor and keep an eye out for a local fortune-teller. She may try to gain access to the hotel."

"What does she look like, sir?"

Gerald didn't know. He turned to Emily, standing just behind him.

"Dark glasses. Mohair coat."

The night porter pointed into the silvery night behind them. "Like that?"

Fragile but determined, as hairy, in her mohair coat in the light of the full moon, as a woman just beginning to turn into a werecreature, there was Madame Nova coming up the path toward them. And yes, she had her dark glasses on.

"Oh my days!" said Peg.

"Quick!" said Gerald. Still at the door, he gestured for his companions to pass him and make for the safety of the hotel bar. "Go! Go! Go!"

"I think we ought to see what she wants," said Dr. Muriel, staying put.

"She looks harmless enough, poor dear," said Peg. "If she's a local psychic, perhaps she wants to talk to me about something?"

Gerald's traffic-cop gestures and staccato shouting had attracted the attention of some of the people at the bar, including Edmund Zenon. "Stay back, Edmund!" said Gerald, noticing his interest. "I'll handle this."

So of course Edmund walked out of the bar and came toward them to see what was going on, followed by Chris, who was followed by the Colonel, who was followed by Hilary and Trina. Tim followed the Colonel. Joseph Seppardi followed Tim. Sarah followed Joseph.

"You!" said Madame Nova as she approached the marble steps leading up to the hotel. "You should be ashamed of yourself. Stay away from me!"

Who did she mean? Emily looked around at the people beside her on the steps outside the hotel, and at the faces inside the hotel, pressed close to the glass doors to see what was going on. It was like walking through customs in an airport, when you know you're not carrying anything illegal, but you still feel guilty. Almost all of them had been in Torquay earlier on, and any one of them might have walked past Madame Nova and given her a fright. Or was there some more sinister, persistent annoyance that she'd had to put up with from one of the guests at the hotel?

"Who do you mean?" Emily asked her. "Has someone been bothering you?"

Madame Nova stood at the bottom of the steps and ignored her. "There's someone here with me. A little girl."

No there wasn't. She was on her own. There was a bit of murmuring to this effect from onlookers.

"She's never far from me. Can you hear her say your name?"

"Oh my God!" someone whispered. "Is it a ghost?"

"You can't hear her, can you? And I'm not sure that I hear her, either," said Madame Nova. "I don't think I remember anymore what her voice was like. I only remember the memories." She looked out across the bay, back in the direction she had come—back at something no one standing here could see. "Traces . . . impressions . . . ephemeral as moonlight silvering the sea in the night."

It was all very theatrical. Emily would have laughed if it hadn't seemed so sad.

Chris edged past the night porter and came to stand on the steps. Edmund came with him. Chris was wrapped up in two thick sweaters after being in the sea. But Edmund was in his shirtsleeves. He shivered.

Chris said to Madame Nova, "Are you all right? Come inside. Come and sit down for a minute."

Madame Nova's gaze was unfocused. She might have been drunk. She pointed into the crowd. "You know what I'm talking about." It wasn't clear who she was addressing. "Her name should be written on your heart." She tottered unsteadily up the steps.

"Come on," said Chris. He and Edmund stepped forward, to take hold of her.

"Leave me alone!" Madame Nova jerked her head back, dark glasses still in place. She lashed out, then stumbled.

Hilary came running from inside the hotel, shoving at Edmund and Chris as they caught hold of Madame Nova. "You heard what she said. Stay away from her!"

There was a tussle as all three of them tried to grab hold of Madame Nova, with Chris and Edmund also trying to avoid manhandling either of the women. Hilary squished Chris's face with the flat of one hand as she tried to push Madame Nova free with the other. Edmund caught hold of Madame Nova in the bosom area with an inadvertent honking gesture and quickly dropped his hand. Madame Nova caught hold of Edmund's breast pocket and fell back, ripping the material and revealing a bare patch of skin on Edmund's chest as she tumbled down the steps.

The murmur went up from the crowd.

"His heart!"

"What is it?"

"I can't see! Is it a tattoo?"

"I think it's a tattoo."

"What's it say? What's written on his heart?"

"There's something written on his heart?"

"What is it? Tell me!"

But there was nothing written there.

Madame Nova lay motionless on the ground at the bottom of the marble steps, Edmund's shirt pocket in her hand. Though it wouldn't suit the myth-making from the chorus on the steps above them, Emily thought Madame Nova had torn the shirt by accident.

"Oh my days!" said Peg. "She's not . . . ?"

"She's alive," said Chris.

"I'll call an ambulance," said Emily.

"No." Madame Nova pushed herself to a sitting position and opened her eyes slowly. Her head hung down awkwardly. "No. I'll just stay here a moment."

"Let's not involve the authorities," said Gerald. He blushed guiltily when he saw Emily looking at him, clearly wondering if the good name of the conference was more important to him than the safety of this vulnerable woman. "If she's uninjured, we should respect her wishes."

"You were in touch with someone, were you?" Peg asked Madame Nova. "A little girl?" Peg crouched down and took her hand. "It's dangerous to make the connection if you're not strong enough mentally."

There were now dozens of people standing awkwardly outside the hotel, either at the top of the steps, or in a semicircle at the bottom of them. Ranald, Marta, Ian, Miriam . . . psychics, skeptics and philosophers, all of them with their names on delegate passes in clear plastic pouches hanging from lanyards around their necks, as if they couldn't be trusted to remember their own names without them.

Sarah also came forward and knelt by Madame Nova, taking her other hand. "We need to get you inside. Do you think you could stand?"

Madame Nova tried to heave herself up. Then she allowed herself to fall back down again, helpless.

"I could give you some healing," Peg offered.

"Would you? That's very kind. It's my leg."

Peg crouched close to Madame Nova and held her hands palm out above her patient's right leg, then she brought her hands together and rubbed them quickly, then she held her palms out again as if warming herself at a brazier. Though it was fascinating to watch, there was nothing about this procedure that indicated to Emily that it would help Madame Nova regain the use of her leg any time soon.

"We need to get her inside," said Gerald. "Before someone calls the police."

"No!" said Madame Nova. "I'll be all right. I'll go home."

"You can't go home," said Peg. "The state of you!"

"I'll fetch the wheelchair," said the night porter. When he had got Madame Nova into it with Chris's help, he wheeled her up the gently sloping ramp at the side of the steps and parked her by the reception desk. Her head hung down. Emily removed her sunglasses gently. Madame Nova's eyes flickered woozily and she exhaled a vapor of Merlot.

The bystanders from outside came back into the hotel, most going upstairs to bed—it was the start of the conference the next day, after all—and a few diehards going back to the bar to keep drinking.

"What if she's got a concussion?" said Peg. "She should stop here tonight."

"We're fully booked," said the porter. "They gave the last two rooms to that family that nearly drowned in the sea."

"She could stay with me," said Sarah. "I've got a spare night-dress. Tim can sleep on the floor."

"If she's like me, she'll be more comfortable in her own bed," said Gerald. "We should order her a taxi."

But the women were in charge of the situation. They weren't going to let Madame Nova go home tonight. "She could stay with me and Trina," said Hilary. "Room ten. We've got a twin room. Trina could sleep in the campervan."

Madame Nova moaned.

Emily said to Madame Nova, "Let's go to the bar and get you some coffee."

"Coffee!" Madame Nova seemed to revive just thinking about it.

Sarah took the handles of Madame Nova's wheelchair and wheeled her toward the bar.

CHAPTER FIFTEEN
A WOMAN IN DANGER

Gerald, Peg, Emily and Dr. Muriel settled in their favorite corner of the bar—"corner" being a notional concept delineated by sofas and chairs in the open-plan arrangement of the ground floor of the hotel. Sarah found herself a chair and parked Madame Nova's wheelchair next to it so she could take care of her.

"Don't you need to be close to your patient, Peg?" Dr. Muriel enquired mischievously.

Peg's response was good humored. "Good thing about this particular style of healing, Muriel, is I can do it medium range. Rum and Coke in one hand, very effective cure for damaged limbs beaming straight to the patient from the other. Now, you don't get that on the National Health Service."

Chris and Tim were sitting with the Colonel at a table nearby, drinking hot toddies. They had collected cardboard beermats from the bar and were collaborating on the construction of a low, box-shaped building on the small table between them, stopping occasionally to debate the dimensions, then add on new rooms and, eventually, an upper floor, also made of beermats. Hilary and Trina sat next to them, watching but not taking part.

"I think next year I might introduce a quiz night on the Friday," said Gerald to Dr. Muriel. "Start building a campus feel from the get-go." He took a picture of his cappuccino and read out the caption he would use for it on Twitter as he tapped it out on his phone: *Hope it won't keep me up all night! Long day ahead tomorrow.* *#BeliefandBeyond*

Emily was writing up her notes about the evening in her notebook, smiling at Gerald's earnestly dull social media updates.

The atmosphere was mellow.

Around them, some of the conference delegates were debating important points they planned to address the following day about the nature of belief; others were just chatting. Bobby Blue Suit was having a nightcap while his dogs slept under a table next to him. A man in a pink polo shirt, with a round face with blue veins in it like Stilton cheese—the conference delegate's pass on the lanyard around his neck identified him as Ian—was trying over and over again to find a coin concealed under one of three leather cups as they were switched around on a low table in front of him by a long-haired man wearing a neckerchief—Romeo, according to the pass around his neck. Romeo had black, collar-length, curly hair. He was wearing a pair of baggy black jeans and a pale green shirt with the sleeves rolled up to just under his elbows, a red handkerchief round his neck and a dark yellow waistcoat on top of the shirt. When he noticed Emily watching him, he winked.

Ian was betting with pennies, the pile of them slowly going lower on his side of the table as they got higher on Romeo's. Ian lost consistently, but on the one occasion he won, he celebrated noisily, tugging at his polo shirt and declaring it his "lucky shirt."

"Astronomer," said Dr. Muriel of Ian in response to the silent question posed by Emily's raised eyebrows.

During the course of the next hour in the bar, people drifted away to bed, or drifted away and came back in again. Miriam Starling, the elegant woman who'd lost her shoe at the last conference, and the German professors, Marta and Birgitte—the delegate passes came in useful for recalling their names—hopped when they passed Dr. Muriel to sit at a table nearby. They laughed as though it was as funny as the first time they did it. Birgitte shook something from a plastic bag with "A Little of What You Fancy" written on it. A rat! Its coat was made of gray fun fur. The paws had pink felt underpads. Its whiskers were stiff, transparent plastic wire. Its tail was very long. Its plastic eyes were wary.

"The professor from Hamelin," said Dr. Muriel. "You probably guessed when you saw the rat? She's doing something about self-fulfilling prophecies at the conference tomorrow, but it's a running joke that whatever she talks about, she'll try to shoehorn in a Pied Piper reference. Some of them do like to use props and running jokes to keep the audience engaged." She waved her silver-topped cane. "I find the threat of a poke in the ribs from this is enough to keep people from falling asleep."

A conference delegate—Philip, so his pass said—approached Dr. Muriel when he saw the cane. "Can I borrow that?" Then he pointed to Edmund's top hat and cloak in a bag on the floor. "And the top hat? I want to do my Fred Astaire."

Dr. Muriel and Edmund handed over the props. "No idea who he is," confided Dr. Muriel to Emily. "Might be a vicar? But if he can dance like Fred Astaire, he'll have won my heart by the morning."

Philip, Ian, Ranald, Marta, Milli, Miriam, Romeo . . . Emily, noting down the names, began to feel like a rookie travel agent giving a muddled-up booking reference over the phone: Romeo, Foxtrot, Hotel, Lima, Miriam . . . There were so many people dipping in and out of her consciousness as part of this conference, and not enough time to get a proper impression of any of them before they drifted off again.

Peg overheard her talking about it with Dr. Muriel. "Well, times that by a hundred and do it with your eyes closed; that's what it's like being a psychic."

Emily had finished writing up Edmund's trick: his disappearance and reappearance, his clever way of using his top hat and cloak as a disguise by removing them, and his immersive theater techniques, putting up posters all over town. Maybe it didn't matter if most of the conference delegates were just names and faces to her. Emily still believed that Madame Nova was at the heart of this somehow, whatever "this" was. It was time to confront her about it.

"Why've you been making predictions about drowning?" Emily asked.

"It was a bit of fun. Just trying to drum up business."

Gerald had been listening. "Funny way to go about it—going around town frightening everyone. Was it you who called the society and suggested we cancel the conference?"

"No," said Madame Nova.

"There was a phone call?" Peg had also been listening. "You know, if you had mentioned it at the time, Gerald, Scotland Yard might not have laughed down the phone at me when I reported my prediction."

Gerald blushed. "I do apologize. I thought it was a crank call."

"You didn't know who it was?" Emily asked him.

Gerald shook his head. "Woman with a low voice."

Madame Nova had a low voice. She kept her mouth shut.

"Never mind, it's over now," said Gerald. "And come Monday we'll have a very interesting report to present to the society. Eh, Emily?"

"A report," said Hilary, eyes on Emily's notebook and pen. "I wondered what you were doing."

"She's writing up the success of my *Psychic Techniques for Future Positivity*," said Peg. She delved into her handbag and brought out a copy of the book, holding it face out to the group in the bar, fingertips curled in so as not to obscure the title, like a presenter on a TV shopping channel.

"Nice work if you can get it, Emily," said Edmund, raising a glass in her direction. "That'll be a very short report."

"It saved *your* hide," snapped Peg.

"Edmund was the one who was supposed to drown," said Sarah. "Isn't that what you told me when we first got here, Emily?"

"Not just drown," said Peg. "Murdered. Choked to death and pulled under the water. My positivity circle deflected the threat."

"What if the murderer's still out there?" Sarah said. "What if he tries to hurt someone else? We need to do something. Joseph, you could find out."

"No, Sarah," Joseph said quietly.

But Sarah wasn't going to drop the idea. She put her hand on Madame Nova's arm. "Maybe that's what your little girl was trying to warn you about just now?"

"I'm a fortune-teller, not a spiritualist, Sarah. The things I do are parlor games. I haven't heard my daughter's voice in years."

"Not everyone has the kind of skill required to connect to the mind of a murderer," agreed Peg.

Edmund stretched out his legs and smiled a languid smile. "There's not *anyone* who has that kind of skill, in my experience, but perhaps someone will change my mind tomorrow."

"Would you be eligible for Edmund's fifty thousand pounds if you could get through tonight?" Sarah asked Peg.

From out in the lobby came the sound of the piano playing. Philip was putting on his top hat. He was tying up his white tie. He was brushing off his tails.

It was Edmund who answered Sarah's question. "No, she wouldn't. We're doing those tests under very strict conditions tomorrow in the Ballroom."

"I shouldn't want it," said Peg, with dignity.

"You wouldn't need it," said Edmund pleasantly. "You'd be famous. You'd be back on TV."

Out in the lobby, Philip was polishing his nails.

By now, most of the conference delegates had gone to bed. Cheese-faced Ian wandered over, looking for entertainment.

"What if nobody wins tomorrow?" said Hilary. "What will you do with the money then?"

"Nothing," said Edmund.

Ian jingled the few remaining coins in his pocket. "Where's the jeopardy? You shouldn't make a wager unless you stand to lose."

"You shouldn't make a wager unless you think you'll win," said Edmund. "But that's not the point. OK, tell you what. If nobody wins, I'll make a donation to charity." He called over to Tim. "What's that charity you're thinking of setting up, in the name of your boy?"

"Liam's Foundation. We might do something in Kenya, with the Colonel."

"I don't want your money," said the Colonel to Edmund. "Wrought from blasphemy."

"I didn't charge anyone to see the trick that you found so blasphemous," said Edmund. "But it's up to you."

"I think we *do* want it," said Tim.

Now Hilary spoke up. "No, you don't."

The Colonel said, "I've made up my mind, Hilary. I'm going to Africa."

"You can't go. We've Trina to think of."

"Why can't I come with you?" Trina looked from the Colonel to Hilary. "Lions and tigers, yeah? I want to come to Africa."

The Colonel smiled at their protégé. "I've had this out with Hilary, many times. It's no place for a woman."

"Forget Africa," Hilary pleaded. "Think of what we could achieve here."

If the Colonel's unsuccessful attempts to baptize people on the beach that afternoon were anything to go by, Emily thought they would probably achieve very little. But she, like everyone else in that corner of the bar, was trying to pretend she wasn't listening.

"It's a sign, meeting Gerald and Tim," said the Colonel. "I'm supposed to go to Africa."

Now Trina weighed in. "You're like God's needy girlfriend. Wanting him to show you he loves you all the time. Wanting a *sign* before you do anything. What sign was it made you almost drown me this afternoon?"

"Trina!" Hilary jogged the table as she half-rose in her seat, knocking over the beermat construction and spilling half an inch out of the top of the drinks that she and Trina had left there.

Tim and the Colonel picked up the scattered beermats. Hilary grabbed the drinks and put them on the floor. Chris found a cloth and mopped up the puddles of orange juice and lemonade on the table. He tried to make a joke of it. "There goes Tim's school in Africa. The big bad wolf has blown your house down, Tim."

"Well, if I'm the big bad wolf," Hilary said as she set the drinks back on the table, "that makes you the three little pigs, then, doesn't it?"

Trina picked up her glass and tipped it up to her mouth, gulping down the fizzy orange mixture. As she drained her drink, she drummed at the leg of her chair with the heel of her boot, absent-mindedly, like a much younger child finishing its bottle of milk and kicking its heels contentedly in its sleepsuit.

Emily wondered how far Trina would have to go back in her life to remember a time when she was happy. Before she was ten? Before she was six? When she was a toddler? When she was a baby drinking milk from a bottle?

Trina set her empty glass down and wiped her mouth with her hand. "I'm going for a bath."

Hilary nodded, barely acknowledging her. She had a question for Edmund. "What happens to the money if something happens to you?"

"Well then, it's null and void. I can't write a cheque if I'm dead, can I?"

"Unless you come through in a séance with your bank details," said Chris.

Edmund grinned at him. "If something happens to me this weekend, you have to *promise* me you'll call on the services of one of our psychic friends. I'll do my best to make an appearance."

Hilary ignored their banter. She put her hand on the Colonel's arm. "What if I could persuade him to go into the water? Would you stay behind then?"

The Colonel was surprised. "You mean Edmund?"

Edmund and Chris thought this was a great joke.

But Hilary was serious. "What if I can save his soul? What if I can make him walk into the water to get blessed?"

Edmund laughed. "Well, then I'd write you a cheque myself, Hilary."

"Why don't you do it now?" she said. "Postdate it and give it to me. If it doesn't happen, you can ask for it back."

There were excited murmurs from the remaining onlookers in the bar. After Edmund's trick that evening, adrenaline levels had begun to lower again, but the body longs for another thrill. The levels were going back up.

"What date would I put on it?" said Edmund. "If you're hoping for a deathbed conversion, I might have spent all the money in my account by then. I'm hoping for a long and eventful life."

"Monday," said Hilary. "Easter Monday. The holiest day in the calendar."

"That's the first of April this year, isn't it?" said Edmund. "It may be the holiest day but it's also, by coincidence this time round, the most amusing." The idea seemed to appeal to him. Perhaps it was only the juxtaposition of the day and the date that made him do it. Perhaps he liked a wager as much as cheese-faced Ian. Each of his tricks and performances was a kind of gamble in its way, after all, Emily thought. He said, "I'll bring the cheque down to breakfast tomorrow—Saturday. You'll have two days to make me see the light. The money's yours, if you can do it. Unless someone gets in before you and proves the existence of the paranormal tomorrow."

"We could set up a church here," said Hilary to the Colonel. "You and me, with your money and the money I get from Edmund. You could preach inside. We'd get hundreds of people coming to listen."

"You're an extraordinary woman, Hilary," the Colonel told her. "I take my hat off to you. For all I know, you might just do it. Heaven knows, you're the one with the ambition and the drive. You're the one who's been doing all the organizing. If you end up with Edmund's money, do something for yourself and Trina with it. Set yourselves up with a nice little home. It's not enough to buy a place, but it'll give you the rent for a few years. Trina could finish school."

"In other words," said Hilary sourly, "you're still going to Africa."

"Look," said Gerald. "Nothing's going to happen to Edmund."

Peg saw an opportunity—finally—to bring the conversation back to herself. "Why don't I make sure? Emily, got your notebook, dear? If Edmund's in any danger—which I very much doubt, given the success of my positivity circle—then I can tune in and find out."

"I want no part of it," said Hilary.

"Nor me," said the Colonel.

Peg ignored them, appealing to the enthusiasts among her small audience. "I have had some success in cases like this in the past, tuning in directly to the mind of the murderer." She didn't give examples. "I'll soon be able to tell you if anyone wishes Edmund any harm."

Joseph Seppardi cleared his throat. They looked over at him. "It's dangerous, what you're suggesting. Opening up a telepathic channel is like any other communication: it's a two-way process. You can listen, but you may not be able to control what you let in."

"Thank you, Joseph. I'll take your concerns on board," said Peg, in the manner of a woman who has been given advice about how to make gravy in her own kitchen. "Ready, Emily?"

Sarah said, "Please don't start without me. I must just pop to the loo."

There were murmurings from various people who thought they might do the same.

Emily watched as Hilary stopped to talk to Madame Nova on her way out of the bar. "You can have Trina's bed tonight, Vivienne. Room number ten. It's close to the elevator, so you'll be able to access it in your wheelchair without too much effort. I'll go and sort out the campervan. Trina can sleep in that if I move the placards."

Vivienne.

"I'm fine," said Madame Nova.

As Sarah had left Madame Nova unattended for a moment, Emily went and sat next to her. "Do you two know each other? You and Hilary."

Madame Nova was more or less sober now, but she looked tired. "I don't want to talk about it."

Which, of course, meant yes.

"Let's have a comfort break," said Peg, "so those who need to can go and spend a penny. Back here in five minutes or we'll start without you."

Women and men scurried off to use the facilities in the hotel—to the lobby, to the spa one level below, or back to their own rooms. Presently they all returned, even the Colonel and Hilary, who took bar stools side by side, far enough away from Peg to make it obvious they disapproved—but close enough to hear what was going on. Joseph Seppardi was there, and Bobby Blue Suit, both taking a professional interest.

"Emily, dear? Ready?" Peg put her palms flat on the arms of her chair. She took a deep breath. "Quiet, please, while I try to connect with a troubled mind."

Emily and Dr. Muriel made eye contact with each other. Dr. Muriel raised her eyebrows, amused. Then Emily opened her notebook and sat with pen poised, ready to take notes.

Peg breathed quietly for about half a minute without speaking. It was quite a long time; it was almost meditative. Emily began to feel sleepy.

Peg said, "I'm getting a woman in danger."

"Oh, Peg." It was Edmund. "Just for once, couldn't you give it a rest?" But he also stayed to watch.

Peg continued, eyes closed. She spoke hesitantly, but with authority. "Might be a girl . . . A young woman, under water."

"You're replaying the events of the afternoon," suggested Gerald. "The near-drowning of the Colonel and the young girl."

Peg said, "I wasn't even there."

"Where is Trina?" said Sarah. "She can't still be in the bath?"

Peg opened her eyes and stared. She looked frightened.

Hilary looked at Peg's stricken face. Then she jumped from her stool and raced through the lobby and up the stairs. Emily and Peg followed her, taking the stairs as fast as they could.

When they reached room number ten, Hilary opened the door and rushed in. As Trina was supposed to be in the bath, Peg and Emily stayed outside to preserve her modesty, heads bent, listening, half-horrified, like nineteenth-century expectant fathers, to what was going on inside. They heard Hilary hammering on the bathroom door and calling out to Trina. Nothing.

They went in and stood next to Hilary. Emily said, "Maybe she's got headphones on? Does she listen to music?"

"On what?" snapped Hilary. "She's a homeless itinerant. She didn't even have a decent toothbrush when I picked her up. Never mind an iPod."

"I'll see if they've something at Reception to open the door." Peg picked up the phone and dialed Reception, but the night porter wasn't answering.

"I'll go and get some of the men from the bar." Emily raced back down the stairs and came back with Chris and the Colonel—and Dr. Muriel, who didn't approve of gender-biased calls for help and came up swinging her cane.

Chris and the Colonel shouldered open the bathroom door, then hung back, slightly embarrassed. Hilary rushed in, the busy midwife, Peg and Emily behind her. The Jacuzzi function on the bath was churning the bubbles up nicely in a full-to-the-brim, cooling bath. No sign of Trina.

Hilary reached in under the foamy water and brought up two white shoulders, topped by a lifeless, lolling head.

"Oh my days!" said Peg, her voice almost a wail. She helped Hilary bring Trina out of the bath, lay her on the floor and wrap her in a towel like a newborn.

"How did you know?" said Hilary.

In the bedroom, Emily heard Chris calling for an ambulance on his mobile phone, saying it might be too late, describing the condition of the girl. It was too late. That word "might" was just Chris's way of trying to keep her in this world.

"How did you know?" Hilary said again.

"I felt it," said Peg. Then she started to cry.

Chapter Sixteen

The Lost Property Office

When they got back to the bar, the atmosphere was chaotic. While paramedics worked in vain upstairs to revive Trina, even before they pronounced her dead and removed the body, people began to speculate about what had happened and why.

"She was a funny little thing. Did she have any family?" Peg asked Hilary. Despite their differing views on the occult, and whether or not Peg was an evil representative of it, Peg and Hilary had been drawn together by the experience of discovering Trina and taking her body from the bath. There was a truce between them now.

"She said not," said Hilary. "No parents alive, anyway. There'll be paperwork to do. I expect the police will try to track down a member of her family."

"You were her carer, were you?" Sarah's eyes were red and her nose swollen where she had been crying. "I admire you for that. Me and Tim thought of fostering after . . . after . . . Poor little lamb! What was she? Couldn't have been more than fifteen?"

"She was nineteen; malnourished and poorly educated, so she seemed younger. I realize that not everyone here will agree with what I have to say, but knowing that she left this life by slipping under the water is quite comforting. It was a tribute to us, I think. To the Colonel. She was accepting a final blessing before she died. She's in a better place."

Trina was in the hospital morgue. She was in the *hell-vote-sluice*. Emily didn't think she was in a better place at all.

Sarah didn't think so, either. "You don't think she did it on purpose?"

"It was an accident, surely?" The Colonel appealed to the room, as if he thought they were accusing him—as if Trina had died earlier that day in the sea, not in the hotel bathroom. "When someone in my care goes under the water, I want them to come back up alive."

"Of course it was an accident," said Hilary.

"Poor little mite," Sarah said. "Peg, you could get in touch with Trina and ask her what happened?"

From the expressions on their faces, both Edmund and Joseph Seppardi thought this was a terrible idea, though for different reasons.

"I'm better at connecting with the minds of the living," Peg admitted. "What did I say about Trina before it happened, Emily? Did you write it down?"

Emily had left her handbag in the bar when she went upstairs. She went over to it now. Her notebook was gone.

"How very odd," said Dr. Muriel. "The receptacle of all your wisdom. You could ask the night porter if it's been handed in."

"I will. And then I need to go to bed." Emily wanted to be alone to recover from the evening's disturbing events.

"I'm not sure I shall sleep tonight," said Dr. Muriel. "I wish I had some sleeping tablets."

Dr. Muriel, who set so much store by the restorative effects of the Torquay sea air? If she was going to resort to sleeping pills, she must be pretty upset, too.

"What brand do you want?" said Peg. "I could let you have a Zopiclone."

"Temazepam, if you need it," said Madame Nova.

"I've got Nightowl," said Sarah, taking a foil blister pack from her handbag. "It's an antihistamine. It's very good."

Dr. Muriel accepted a Nightowl tablet and carried it in her hand with her on her way up to bed.

Sarah took hold of the handles of Madame Nova's wheelchair. "You want to stay with me tonight? I'll put Tim in with Joe." She pushed her new friend toward the elevator, not waiting for an answer.

◆ ◆ ◆

Emily's small bedroom in the eaves would have been filled with ghosts if she believed in them—the hotel's promotional literature explained that wounded soldiers had been housed in the rooms on the top floor during the Second World War. But Emily wasn't thinking of ghosts. She went to sleep and dreamed of drowning.

She saw Trina in a white dress, standing up to her chest in the waves, cursing Edmund Zenon in a language Emily didn't understand. Given her lack of education, Trina probably wouldn't understand it, either. But this was a dream, and dreams have their own logic. Trina put her hand up in a fist and tapped on the air in front of her with her knuckles, *toc toc, toc toc*, to attract Emily's attention. Emily turned over in bed. If Trina was going to drown in front of her, she didn't want to see it. Then Trina opened her mouth and began to make an inarticulate sound like a car alarm, with a persistent wail. *Wah WAH! Wah WAH! Wah WAH!* Trina was trying to warn Emily about something. But what?

She woke to realize she wasn't developing psychic powers that were enabling her to communicate with the dead. The sound she was hearing was the bedside telephone, not a car alarm. The person who was trying to reach her was not Trina but one of the staff at the hotel, calling to tell her that her notebook had been taken to the Lost Property Office if she'd like to come down for it. Emily checked the time on her mobile phone. Three o'clock in the morning! The notebook could wait.

But she couldn't get back to sleep. She decided to go down and fetch the notebook. She wanted to write down her thoughts about what had happened to Trina, to try to make sense of it.

Emily got dressed and went downstairs. She felt bleary eyed and groggy. The hotel was eerily dark and quiet. She felt none of the excited anticipation she had felt as she checked into her room earlier that day. The emptiness was disconcerting, the shadows malevolent.

She went to Reception but the night porter was not there. He had left a note to say he was doing his rounds and would be back shortly. There was a number to dial for anyone wanting urgent attention. Ah well. She was heading back to her room when she saw him coming out of the Ballroom. She asked about the notebook.

"I didn't call you."

"No. It was a woman. She said it had been handed in to Lost Property."

"That's down by the spa in the basement. I'd have to unlock it for you."

"Do you mind?"

He probably did mind. But he said it was no trouble at all. Emily reflected that if she were a night porter she'd be glad of interruptions in the long, boring nights, so she didn't feel bad about troubling him. But then, as he led the way down the steps to the basement, she thought that he probably had a really good book to read and then she was sorry for disturbing him.

There was a strong smell of chlorine as they passed the spa with its Jacuzzi and decent-size swimming pool, the blue water lit up even at night. If Emily could have one wish (after world peace), it would be to have the use of a private swimming pool. If she had a pool at home, she could come down at night and swim in the blue-lit darkness alone, instead of negotiating the lanes at the local public pool, clogged with splashy showoffs and slow zigzaggers, and with balls of hair and lost contact lenses drifting along the bottom.

The Lost Property Office was an inviting jumble of umbrellas, false limbs, false teeth, paperback books, mobile phones, keys, cuddly toys, socks and coats. Emily could have spent all night in there examining each item and trying to guess the story of how it had ended up here. But when she turned to the porter to make some remark about the contents of this treasure trove, she could see he didn't share her fascination. Perhaps more importantly, there was no sign of her notebook.

The night porter locked up again without saying *I told you so.* "Do you know your way back up to the lobby? Got to finish doing my rounds." He pointed his thumb in the other direction, to show where he was headed.

Emily did know the way. She also knew that if you were exploring a haunted house—or a haunted hotel—you should never split up. But she had put the poor man to enough trouble already. And this place wasn't haunted, just a bit creepy at night. As she approached the spa and saw the blue glow of the pool, it now seemed less like an unattainable luxury and more like the kind of place where a mad scientist would incubate experimental monstrosities. And then . . . and then her head hurt and it all went black. But not before Emily had time to remember, absurdly, that Bobby Blue Suit had told her to call for Shirley if she was ever in trouble. What good would that do? She pictured Shirley's long, glossy auburn coat. She pictured Shirley's long, inquisitive nose, her intelligent brown eyes and her extremely short legs. *Run and get help, Shirley!* How long would that take? There was a reason why they didn't have miniature dachshunds working for the emergency services.

Blackness. Had she fainted?

Not awake, not dead, not dying, not sleeping. What was this sensation? She had flown before in dreams. She wasn't flying. She was moving. She could smell chlorine. Was she swimming? She wasn't swimming. She was being dragged along the floor.

She could hear barking. She thought of her dog, Jessie. What would Jessie think if she knew she had been passed off as a spirit guide and Emily a paranormal investigator? But Jessie had never formed an opinion about anything Emily had said unless the words *dinner, walk* or *treat* appeared in the sentence.

A wet nose, snuffling, warm furry ears, licking sounds, the tinkling of a name tag against the metal buckle of a collar, prawny breath. Either Emily had died and gone to heaven and Jessie was there—in which case yay for there being dogs in heaven—or Jessie had reappeared on earth, in which case yay for unexplained paranormal events. Or maybe there was another explanation? One which eluded Emily momentarily.

"Shirley!"

Is my name Shirley? I think it might be. It's something like that.

"Shirley! Oh my goodness, Emily!"

No, it's Emily. That's it.

"Emily, you've fainted, doll." A man's voice. "Don't try to get up. Stay still a minute. Can you open your eyes? Oi, Elvis, will you get away from that! Stop licking that blood."

Emily kept her eyes closed. "Is it my blood?"

"You've cut your head where you went down. Good luck you didn't go six inches further or you'd have been headfirst into the pool. Eddie! It's not a butcher's shop! It's poor Emily's blood. These dogs, honestly. They get me up at least once every night for a tiddle. Worse than having a baby. Still, if I hadn't been passing, you'd have been there for hours, I'm guessing. You were sparked out cold. Did you want me to call a doctor, or can you sit up?"

Emily sat up and opened her eyes. She saw Bobby Blue Suit and his dogs, so she knew her sight was OK. She touched her head. There was a cut by her eye which was bleeding, and a painful lump on the back of her head. The lump was the size and shape of an egg when she touched it. "It's hot in here."

"I expect that's what made you faint. You've been rushing around, up and down stairs. Then that business with the dead body."

Emily remembered what had happened to Trina. She began to cry.

Bobby bent to hug her. "Awww, bless you. Delayed shock." His three dogs tried to jump in his lap as he crouched down to comfort Emily, wagging their tails and nudging each other for the best position. "What were you doing down here? Not thinking of going skinny-dipping?"

"I can't have been going to the pool. Can I? I do like swimming . . . I can't remember, Bobby. I was in the bar . . ."

"I saw you in there. I don't remember you drinking. You're not drunk, are you?"

"I don't know."

"I'll take you to the hospital. Shouldn't be too long to wait in Accident and Emergency this time of night. Not in Torquay. Mind you, Friday night is fall-down-drunk-and-split-your-head-open night in most country towns, so I could be wrong."

"I'm OK. I don't need stitches, do I?"

Bobby peered at the cut on her head. "No. That'll heal up nicely. You'll get a nasty bruise, mind."

She was cold and wet from lying on the tiles by the side of the pool. "You know what? I'm just going to go up to bed. Thanks, Bobby."

"I hope we won't get into trouble for being by the pool. Animal fur and streaks of blood, it looks like a fox has been after a chicken in here. Eddie and Elvis have taken care of most of the blood. Maybe we can blame the fur on a hirsute guest."

As they went up the stairs, Emily thought she owed Bobby one thing at least. "You told me I should call Shirley if I was in trouble. Do you remember? I did think of her as I went down, just before I hit the tiles."

"And next thing you knew, you saw Shirl. Aw, I'm glad you told me, Emily."

Emily was glad, too, when she saw how happy it made him. And then, when she was treated to five minutes of Bobby's special dog voice as he congratulated Shirley for being so clever, she began to regret it. Almost everyone who has a dog also has a dog voice that they use to communicate with their pet. Too often it's a baby-talk voice, incorporating lots of silly made-up words, and it should never be used in public, especially not when climbing the stairs of a historic hotel with a crying, bleeding, snot-nosed girl who thinks she has just fainted and doesn't know the half of it.

Chapter Seventeen
Why?

Emily woke up with blood on her pillow, a cut lip, a cut and swollen right cheek, and a black eye. She stepped gingerly out of bed and hobbled to the bathroom to look in the mirror, where she saw a prizefighter face. With her fingertips, she felt the tender egg-shaped lump on the back of her skull. It was huge! And painful to touch. Her mouth was dry and she had a groggy, hungover feeling. Was she a bit dizzy? Yes, probably. But she would live. When she was at home in London, whenever she had to run for the bus, she was glad she wasn't an international spy, running, running, running all over the place to get away from danger. Now she was glad she wasn't really a future crimes investigator, with a badge and a gun and enemies, getting beaten up all the time. Come Tuesday morning she'd be back to work in an office and, though the work was boring, at least it wasn't painful. Nobody ever died of boredom, no matter how many claimed they thought they might.

It was Saturday, the start of the conference, the big day for Edmund's paranormal challenge. Fortunately it was still early—there was something important she had to do before anything else. She had a shower and washed her hair and washed the blood off her face, and then she got dressed and went downstairs.

She tried to sneak past Mandy Miller at Reception, but Mandy wanted a chat. "Whatever happened to you? Are you all right?"

"I fainted last night. I'm a bit dizzy, but I'll be all right." Emily touched the lump on the back of her head to see if it had got any bigger. She thought perhaps it had.

"Dehydration. That's what made you faint. Too many people think they're hungry when they're thirsty, then they keel over. Happened to my sister in Tesco and she went headfirst and knocked over their Easter egg display. They wanted to make her pay for it. Thought she was drunk! Make sure you drink plenty of water today. You want me to call a doctor?"

Emily smiled and shook her head, very slowly.

"Terrible about that girl, wasn't it? Much too young to take her own life." Mandy leaned forward and spoke in a confidential whisper, so Emily had to lean in to hear what she had to say. "I wondered if it was mind control. Someone took over her mind and made her do it."

"That's quite a theory. Is there somewhere round here I can buy dog treats?"

"The Pound Shop. It's two streets down on the left. You can get two big bags for—"

"OK!"

"For a pound."

"Thank you." Emily went through the glass doors into the early morning air.

♦　♦　♦

When she got back to the hotel, Emily joined Dr. Muriel and Gerald for breakfast in the dining room. They were at a large table near the window overlooking the sea, scoffing down bacon, eggs and sausages, mushrooms, toast and grilled tomatoes. Dr. Muriel's hair was wet from her morning swim. Gerald was engrossed in the crossword in his newspaper. He gasped when he looked up and saw Emily's injured face. He and Dr. Muriel winced sympathetically as she told them how she came by her injuries.

At nearby tables, the academics who had come to take part in the conference were making last-minute amendments to their speeches, fueling themselves for the day with plates piled high with waffles, pancakes, omelettes and, of course, the nation's favorite: the full English breakfast. Emily, a vegetarian, was eating sheep's yoghurt with honey. It seemed that she was the only one in the dining room who saw the breakfast buffet as an invitation rather than a challenge.

"It's just as well the meals are included at a set rate in the hotel's conference package," said Gerald, holding his newspaper flat and filling in seven across in his crossword with a pencil. "These people would bankrupt us otherwise."

Joseph Seppardi was having a whispered argument with Sarah and Tim at the next table. "I won't do it!"

The three of them were with Madame Nova, still in her wheelchair. Whereas Sarah, Tim and Joseph were animated, whispering fiercely among themselves, it seemed that someone had forgotten to switch Madame Nova on. Her head hung slackly and she had not touched any of the food Sarah had fetched from the buffet and put in front of her. She was dressed flamboyantly in a faux leopard-skin cloak with a faux fur trim around the hood, and sunglasses. But the outfit contrasted with the desiccated body within, a dried corncob dressed up for the Mexican Day of the Dead. It was impossible not to stare at that outfit, though for politeness' sake Emily pretended to be looking instead at the condiments that had been set in the middle of the table: the miniature bottle of tomato ketchup, the jars of horseradish sauce and English mustard, the salt and pepper. But even staring at those yielded a reward because, as Sarah struggled with the tomato ketchup bottle—it was apparently new and had never been opened—Madame Nova snatched it from her, wordlessly, and twisted the top off it effortlessly before giving it back. Impressive!

Emily wasn't the only one fascinated by their breakfast arrangements. "Excuse me," Gerald said, leaning over to take a picture of Tim's brimful breakfast plate. "Do you mind? I forgot to do this before I started eating." He put the photo up on Twitter. *Great start to the conference. Full English breakfast. And a full day ahead. #BeliefandBeyond.*

"No sign of Peg?" asked Emily.

"Perhaps last night was too much for her," said Gerald. "She was very upset. And if *you're* feeling dizzy from running up and down the stairs, then think of the toll it must have taken on Peg. She's a big woman and she has a few years on you."

"Should I go and look for her? Make sure she's all right?"

"Let her rest," said Gerald. "If she's anything like me, she won't want to be disturbed by a knock on the door or a phone call if she's asleep."

"Oh," said Emily, remembering. "I got a phone call last night while I was asleep. *That's* why I went downstairs."

"Morning!" Edmund turned up from the breakfast buffet with two croissants balanced on his plate. "Blimey, Emily! I hope the other fella came off worse." He took a seat next to Gerald and tapped at an unsolved clue in Gerald's cryptic crossword. "Nine down is Albert Camus."

Chris—buttermilk pancakes and mixed seasonal berries—raised his eyebrows sympathetically at the state of Emily's battered face.

"I still don't know exactly how you did that trick," Emily said, to steer the conversation away from her hideous injuries.

"Just between us?" Edmund smiled. "It's impossible for a man to walk on water, isn't it? And it's impossible for a man to get from place A to place B in the wink of an eye—"

"Took a bit longer than that last night," said Chris.

"Were there two men?" Emily looked from Edmund to Chris. "Two men of a similar build. One in place A, one in place B, both wearing a top hat and a cape. The one in place A takes advantage of an apparent fault with the flickering lights to discard the recognizable clothing and hide in the water. The one in place B gets dressed up and shows himself."

Edmund and Chris grinned at her, though they didn't say she was right.

Gerald pushed his plate away. "It was a clever trick, gentlemen. I'm sure you could have got more people to see it if you'd told people to be at the pier for 7:00 p.m."

"Advertising the start time would have formalized it," said Chris. "People would have been prepared for the trick, looking to see if it was any good, trying to guess how it worked. But because they seemed to stumble on it, first they were asking what they were seeing, then they were inviting others to come and look—and telling each other they had to be quick because it was happening *now* and it would be over soon. The people who were doing that had become involved. The outcome was important to them; they wanted other people to see what they were seeing and share in the experience. They felt they were part of it. So they weren't walking up and down looking for the joins, they were too busy telling other people what they should expect to see. They helped set the stage for us. Half the people who'll be talking about it today won't even have seen it, but they'll feel like they did. The people who did see it will exaggerate, to make what they saw seem more spectacular, their experience more worthwhile, their memory more valuable." He shrugged, pleased with himself. "Who says you need a TV or a computer to broadcast an experience like this? You can transmit it from brain to brain, from mouth to mouth, with a bit of planning."

"So this wasn't about the trick, so much as what happened around it?" Emily asked.

"You got it, Emily." Edmund smiled at her, enjoying the opportunity to talk about his work. "And we won't be able to measure how successful it was until a few days from now—maybe even as far away as next year—when we come back and find out whether everyone's still talking about it."

"I don't think we'll be coming back to Torquay with Belief and Beyond," said Gerald. "I'm hoping to get sponsorship to hold it in Dubai."

"Good idea." Madame Nova creaked into life again—she and Tim and Sarah and Joseph had all been listening. "Go wherever you like with it. Just don't come back to Torquay."

There was a polite silence while everyone waited to see if she had anything more to contribute. She didn't. So they turned back to Edmund.

He smiled a subdued version of his charming smile. "Ach, look. It doesn't seem right to keep talking about my trick. I want to celebrate, but that kid last night, Trina . . ."

"I need cheering up," said Dr. Muriel.

"We all do," said Sarah.

Edmund's reticence was genuine, but the words soon came tumbling out as he looked from face to face, sharing his enthusiasm about the success of the trick. "The whole event was a kind of enhanced storytelling. When you listen to someone tell a story, it can be a compelling experience, can't it? But here, instead of one storyteller, we get dozens, all embellishing the same truth, all helping to make the experience more exciting for friends and strangers by adding their own little flourishes to the tale. Chris's idea. I'd consulted him about some of the street theater aspects of the show—how we were going to handle the discoverability, create the buzz. When my technical manager was called away at short notice, Chris was a natural choice. There aren't many people who could do this job. But I knew Chris and trusted him. If I didn't have Chris, I couldn't have done the trick."

"The whole thing was a performance. And the great thing was that half the town had the chance to take part and make it into something special." Chris smiled as he looked around the table, though there was a sympathetic downward hitch of his mouth as he took in Emily's bruises.

"Two lumps," said Dr. Muriel, stirring her coffee thoughtfully.

Emily passed her the white china bowl filled with cubes of white and brown sugar, wondering why it was only fancy hotels that served sugar like that.

"Not the sugar. Two lumps on your head. If you got that one on your cheek when you hit the floor as you went down, then why have you got one on the back of your head?"

"How do you know about the one on the back of my head?"

"You keep touching it to see if it hurts, and then scrunching up your face because it does. I was wondering when you'd learn to stop touching it—I think we'd get quicker results with monkeys in a lab, though I don't believe in experimenting on animals, so we'll never know—and then I started wondering why you had two lumps."

"What is the explanation?" asked Gerald with a scientist's interest. "Did she bounce?"

"She was hit on the back of the head," Dr. Muriel said. "That's why she fell. She didn't faint. She feels dizzy because she got a bump on the head, not the other way round."

"Does it feel as though you were hit?" Chris asked Emily. He stood up and walked round to the back of her chair.

"Honestly? I've never been hit on the back of the head before so I can't say. I've never been hit anywhere, ever, not even play fighting when I was a child. It felt like I fainted. I lost consciousness."

"I'm not surprised. You got hit quite hard." Chris touched the back of her head very gently, which felt wrong for all sorts of reasons. Emily shivered.

"Why would someone lure me down to the swimming pool and hit me over the head? To frighten me off? Off what? I have no idea what's going on. I lost my notebook as well last night."

"I wonder if the two things are connected," said Dr. Muriel. "Peg was talking you up last night, saying how important that notebook was. To anyone listening—to anyone intending to do harm—it could seem that it was full of clues to their identity."

"But no one's been harmed," said Gerald.

"Haven't they? What about Trina?"

"Suicide, surely. Look, Muriel, don't go putting these ideas about. You'll frighten the delegates."

Dr. Muriel ignored him and addressed Emily. "What if the intention wasn't to frighten you but to drown you because of what you knew? You said Bobby and his dachshunds found you. They must have disturbed your attacker before he or she could dump you in the water."

"Well, if I was a target because of my notebook, then what about Peg? She was the one who . . ."

No need to finish that thought. Emily and Dr. Muriel stood up from the table. Dr. Muriel unhooked her silver-topped walking stick from the back of her chair and held it in front of her like a staff.

Gerald got out his phone.

"Gerald, really! This is no time for Twitter," Dr. Muriel told him.

But he wasn't on Twitter. He was calling Peg. He put the phone to his ear when the call connected. But he shook his head to let them know it had gone to voicemail. "Are you going to her room? I'll go with you," he said.

"I'll go," said Chris.

"No," said Emily. "Gerald might be right. Perhaps she's just having a lie-in. We'll come and fetch you if we need your help."

First they went to the reception desk to ask Mandy Miller to call Peg's room. When there was no answer, Mandy got a master key and took them up there.

The generous-sized bedroom was empty. The double bed was neatly made, as though it hadn't been slept in. There was a suitcase on the floor, with a handbag on top of it and a pair of shoes beside it. A paisley scarf was draped on an armchair. So far as Emily could tell, the room had been occupied but the occupant had vanished. There was no sign of a struggle.

Emily looked at Dr. Muriel and Mandy, then she walked the few paces to the adjoining bathroom and pushed the door open, keeping her body as far back from the doorway as possible, as if something—or someone—might jump out at them.

As the door swung inwards, they stepped back, frightened, though there was no one in there who could hurt them. Peg was lying in a bath full of water, fully clothed, staring straight at them. She was dead.

◆　◆　◆

While Mandy went into the bedroom to call the police and the hotel manager, Emily tried to take in as much information as possible before the place was sealed off as a crime scene.

"A heart attack?" asked Dr. Muriel.

"It looks like she's been strangled. Look at the burst blood vessels in her eyes."

Emily and Dr. Muriel leaned in and inspected the body with their hands behind their backs, like well-behaved children in a museum, so as not to disturb the evidence.

"No scratches or bruises. You see that red line round her neck, though, Emily?"

"Someone came right up to her and choked her with *something*—and she let them do it without putting up a fight."

"A ghost?" Mandy had edged back into the bathroom, half turned away so she didn't have to look at Peg's body. "A supernatural being? Or . . . someone takes control of her mind and she lets them do whatever they want with her?"

Dr. Muriel smiled politely. "Interesting. But I'm not convinced by that theory. Emily?"

"The bath was filled after Peg got in it."

Dr. Muriel and Mandy were impressed by this. "How do you know?"

"She may not have put up a fight as her killer came toward her, but her limbs would have jerked and she'd have struggled as she died, wouldn't she? But there's no water splashed on the floor."

Dr. Muriel shook her head sadly. "What does it mean, I wonder?"

"I don't know. I can't see what she was choked with, can you? Could be a belt or a pair of tights or anything."

They looked on the floor of the bathroom but there was no obvious murder weapon. That was it; their last chance to look and try to determine what had happened, because the hotel manager arrived to shoo them out and lock the door, ready for the police to come.

◆　◆　◆

They went back to the restaurant to tell Gerald and the others what had happened.

Gerald loosened his tie. He picked up his napkin and fanned his face with it. He had gone a horrible gray color.

"Put your head between your knees," suggested Dr. Muriel.

"I'm OK. I just can't believe Peg's gone." Gerald's hands trembled. "You're sure it couldn't have been accidental? A heart attack?"

"No," said Emily. "It looked as though she'd been strangled. I'm not sure how. There was no sign of a cord or anything nearby. We looked. Whoever did it must have taken it with them when they left the room."

"Well, then surely they'd have been noticed, walking around the hotel with a noose." Gerald was babbling. It was the shock setting in.

"They wouldn't have to be carrying something that looked like a noose. It could be . . ." Emily looked around the room for inspiration. There was Bobby Blue Suit with his dachshunds. He smiled at her and waved. "It could be something innocuous, like a dog's lead."

Dr. Muriel eyed the elegant gray-, green- and blue-striped tie that Gerald had just loosened. "When one looks, one begins to see all sorts of possible murder weapons."

"Are you going to cancel the conference?" asked Edmund.

"There are so many people here," said Gerald. "How can I? What would I say to them?"

Edmund wasn't impressed. "You could say that two women have died, and that's more important than your conference. Tell everyone to go home, Gerald."

Emily stuck up for Gerald. "There's no point doing that. The police will tell everyone to stay here while they make their enquiries, anyway." Somewhat illogically, she was annoyed with Edmund for being alive—she must have been in shock, too. "Two women have died, yet you were the one who was supposed to drown, according to Peg's premonition—or she thought it was you, anyway.

Something's . . . I don't know. There are plenty of clues but I can't make sense of any of them."

"Clues?" Edmund smirked.

"Emily," said Gerald kindly, "it's not your fault that Trina and Peg have died. You weren't supposed to be here to prevent Edmund's death—or theirs, for that matter. You only have to make a report. Just write up Peg's prediction and its outcome."

The Colonel and Hilary came to join them. Ordinarily, they could have expected special treatment—after all, Trina had died the night before. But, with their competing grief for Peg, everyone at Emily's table greeted them rather numbly.

"I need to get out," said the Colonel when he heard about Peg. "I need to do something. I need to wash away this evil. I need to go down to the water's edge and find someone who will accept God's blessing."

"Do you have that cheque for me, Edmund?" Hilary asked him.

"Hilary!" said the Colonel. Hilary's face shut down, wiping the expression from itself like an Etch A Sketch.

But Edmund laughed and took his chequebook from the back pocket of his jeans. "April the first?" he said, as he wrote the date on it.

Hilary nodded and put out her hand for it.

"I'm tempted to say, 'I'll see you in hell first.' But I don't believe in it."

"I do," said Hilary as she tucked the cheque into her purse.

"Come on," said Dr. Muriel to Emily. "We've got a little time before the conference starts. Let's go into one of the meeting rooms and use one of the whiteboards to get our clues unmuddled." She shot a quick look at Edmund, to see if he was going to challenge her about her use of the word *clues*. He was too distracted by Hilary. "We'll throw out thoughts at random, write the most interesting ones up on a board on the wall. Standard procedure when I'm trying to brainstorm a theory with my students. Soon we'll have something useful to work with, you'll see. It's our best chance until you recover your notebook."

◆ ◆ ◆

So Emily and Dr. Muriel went to the Winston Churchill room. Chairs had been laid out ready for the conference that morning, with overhead projectors, whiteboards and flip charts set up in the room. A fresh pack of chunky red, blue, black and green marker pens had been supplied with each flip chart. A thick black pen and an eraser had been set out with each whiteboard. Everything was neat and orderly as it should be. But this left the question of who had drawn the obscene picture of a man's private parts on the whiteboard.

Dr. Muriel attempted to wipe it off, but unfortunately the artist had used one of the permanent markers supplied with the flip charts, rather than the wipeable whiteboard pens. The picture would have to remain there until the offices of the local supplier of conference equipment reopened after the Easter weekend and some special solvent was brought from Exeter.

"Never mind, we'll use this," said Dr. Muriel, flipping back the cover of a flip chart pad with a flourish and taking up a pen. "Now, what are your thoughts about the drownings?"

But Emily wasn't able to articulate her thoughts. She was distracted by the picture on the whiteboard.

With the sigh of a woman who has done this many times before in one classroom or another over the years, Dr. Muriel turned to the whiteboard, pen in hand, and prepared to transform the picture into something less distracting. She began to add a few artistic flourishes of her own. But just then a porter shouldered open the door, a jug of water in each hand. He took one look at the obscenity that confronted him and deduced, not unreasonably, that Dr. Muriel was responsible for it. He shot a jaded, seen-it-all-because-I-work-in-a-hotel look at Emily and backed quietly out of the room.

Job done, Dr. Muriel returned to the flip chart. Behind her, the whiteboard now depicted a space rocket—with "#BeliefandBeyond" written up the side—propelled from a launchpad toward the stars by two great balls of fire.

"Now, what are your thoughts about the drownings, Emily?"

"It all seems to have begun with Madame Nova. No . . . it seems to have begun with the posters. Edmund Zenon walking on water. As soon as she saw those, Madame Nova started emailing Peg and their network psychics, and I'm pretty sure she called Gerald, too, though she denies it."

"But was she threatening them or warning them?"

"I don't know. I'll tell you something else interesting. She and Hilary are connected somehow. Hilary called her 'Vivienne' like they were old friends."

"What *is* Hilary up to with that postdated cheque? She can't seriously believe she'll get Edmund to walk into the water? It would help our case enormously if one could say that as soon as Madame Nova saw that poster, she knew her old friend Hilary would be down here making a wager with Edmund that she could get him to walk into the water, and she wanted to warn him off in case he drowned."

"Wouldn't it! Except he hasn't drowned. And what about Peg and Trina? Who strangled Peg? It would have to be someone strong." Emily thought of Madame Nova twisting the metal top off a new tomato ketchup bottle without first running it under hot water and then bashing it with a knife.

"Not that strong, if they'd drugged their victim first. You were in the bathroom when Peg and Hilary pulled Trina out of the water, but I stayed in the bedroom. Yes? Well, there was an empty bottle of sleeping pills on the bedside table. A classic suicide, you may say. But there was no note. Just the empty bottle with the label turned out. It seemed staged to me."

"So that's why you were asking about sleeping pills last night."

"You noticed! I wondered if someone had slipped them to her; if Trina could have taken them unknowingly. Or if someone had talked her into taking them—young women can be very fragile, emotionally. Poor Trina would have been susceptible if someone had tried to destroy what was left of her self-esteem. But most of the women had a supply of tablets, so that didn't get me anywhere." Dr. Muriel turned to her flip chart, pen in hand. She hadn't yet written anything on there. "We could do a timeline to find out who had the opportunity to get to Trina and feed pills to her or persuade her to take them."

"I'm not sure there's any point doing a timeline—nearly everyone left the bar at some point last night after Trina had gone upstairs. And that doesn't help us find out what happened to Peg. Anyone staying at the hotel could have gone to her room last night while everyone else was asleep. And Madame Nova conveniently fell down the steps, so she had to stay at the hotel. I still think all this is something to do with Madame Nova."

"Did she fall? Or was she pushed? Hmm? Hilary gave her a good shove while she was 'rescuing' her from Edmund and Chris—did you notice?"

"You're right. But why? Was she trying to keep her away from the hotel, or find an excuse for her to stay here? You think they could be in this together?"

"Well, let's not close down our list of suspects too soon. Did you see anyone wandering about while you were looking for your notebook in the early hours of the morning? Preferably, as Gerald put it, someone wandering around with a noose."

"Only the night porter. And Bobby Blue Suit."

"Bobby and Madame Nova working together?" asked Dr. Muriel. "What do you think?"

"If Hilary and Madame Nova were working together, that would make more sense."

"What about Hilary and the Colonel? He's certainly very keen on submerging people in water."

Emily's hand went to the bump on the back of her head. Could the Colonel be the monster who had sent one woman—perhaps two—to her grave? Could he have strangled Peg and filled her bath? Could he have drowned Trina in her bubbles? Could he have been about to do the same to her in the pool when Bobby Blue Suit and his dogs interrupted him?

"He seems to be in a hurry to get to Africa," said Dr. Muriel. "Did you hear him tell Hilary it was no place for a woman?"

"When he said it's no place for a woman, I think he meant it's no place for Hilary."

Dr. Muriel laughed. "Perhaps you're right. What about Joseph Seppardi? I'm not sure what to make of him. It seems Sarah's signed him up for the paranormal challenge, but he doesn't want to do it. Yet when he 'made contact' with Liam, it seems the boy wanted them to come here. If he doesn't want to do Edmund's challenge, he must have some other reason for being in Torquay."

"Unless he's for real."

"Joseph Seppardi?" Dr. Muriel laughed at that, too. "Look, I need to get to the Ballroom in a minute. But here's a question for you: If Edmund was supposed to die when he did his walking-on-water trick, then why didn't he?"

"Apart from the influence of Peg's positivity circle, you mean?" Emily couldn't quite laugh at that, with Peg so recently dead. She and Dr. Muriel exchanged a rueful smile. "Well, Chris stepped in at short notice because Edmund's technical manager was called away to Brazil—Edmund said he couldn't have done the trick without him. So maybe someone was planning to sabotage it, but Chris prevented it from happening."

"Chris as a one-man version of Peg's positivity circle? That's a very nice idea. He's a dear boy. I like him ever so much, don't you?" Dr. Muriel beamed. "Well, I'm so glad we've done this. It's been very useful, don't you think?"

But all she had written on the flip chart was: Why?

Chapter Eighteen
He's Not Worth It

At the hotel reception, Emily told Mandy Miller she was thinking of booking a ticket to Rio de Janeiro.

"You want Fly Me to the Moon just off the High Street," Mandy told her. "Ask for Dawn, she'll give you a discount." She held up a notebook. "Is this yours? Cleaners handed it in this morning."

"Thank you!" Emily was relieved and only *slightly* offended that whoever had stolen it—if it had been stolen—hadn't seen anything important enough in it to destroy it or do a better job of hiding it. "I got a call in the middle of the night to say it was in the Lost Property Office. But when I went down to the basement, it wasn't there."

Mandy's eyes widened. "You heard *a voice in the night* that told you to go down to the basement?"

Emily laughed. "It wasn't like that."

"However did you find the Lost Property Office anyway?"

"The night porter showed me."

Mandy stared at her blankly.

Emily wondered if she was using incorrect terminology. "The guy on Reception last night, wearing the hotel livery. He showed me where it was."

"A night porter? In a uniform? We haven't had one of those since the Second World War!"

Now it was Emily's turn to stare. Had she seen a ghost? But hadn't the same night porter been on duty when she'd come back to the hotel with everyone else? Emily looked back through the memories she had created last night, trying to remember.

"Nah! Just kidding about the night porter. That'll be Len, probably. Sorry. I couldn't help myself. I do love a good ghost story. Used to work in a place with a headless knight in armor that walked around clanking. Never saw it personally but them who did said it's not as scary as it sounds once you get used to it."

Clanking? Emily smiled gamely.

"If you don't mind me saying, it sounds like you weren't yourself when you went downstairs. Like someone did a mind hack on you. Did it feel like that? Like someone getting remote access to your computer? Like, you're sitting there, logged into Facebook, and you're watching the screen, and someone's typing something on your status update, *and it isn't you!*"

"You think I was brainwashed?"

"Could be. There'd have been a trigger sound to make you obey their command. Remember anything?"

"There was the sound of the phone ringing. And before that . . . a tapping sound. Kind of *toc toc, toc toc*. But I don't think I've been brainwashed. I think I was just tired; not thinking properly. It's not like you've got the CIA staying here."

Mandy stared at her as if this was a particularly stupid thing to say. "We've got the Belief and Beyond conference going on, yeah? It's, like, *full* of people who are hypnotists."

But Emily didn't think she'd been hypnotized. She didn't think Peg had been hypnotized, and nor had Trina. Someone had used something real and heavy to knock her out last night. And before that, before any of them had even arrived in Torquay, someone— maybe the same person, maybe not—had used a real-world solution to get Edmund's technical manager out of the way. Emily had a hunch who it was, even if she didn't know why. She walked down the hill trying to think of cunning ways to trap Dawn into answering her questions. She didn't anticipate that she would soon be trying to think of ways to get Dawn to stop talking.

"Mandy Miller sent me here," Emily told Dawn, who was sitting in front of a computer screen that she had personalized by sticking an orange-haired plastic troll on top of it.

"You up at the hotel, then? Terrible what's happened, isn't it?" Dawn picked up her phone and checked the screen before putting it back on her desk, disappointed. "You'd never know it from Twitter, though. That hashtag, #BeliefandBeyond, it's all pictures of what dinner they've had and, 'Ooh, here's my sausages and egg I had for breakfast.' If you want the gossip, don't bother following *them*."

"I wanted to ask you about flights. A friend of mine got a very good deal on a ticket to Rio recently. I wondered if you could match it. I think she might have bought it from you."

"Oh yeah?" Dawn sat back in her swivel chair and gave Emily a knowing look. Emily thought she was busted. She was going to get a lecture about client confidentiality. But Dawn said, "Madame Nova's a friend of yours, is she?"

"Not a friend, exactly. She did offer to tell my fortune."

Dawn laughed at that. "She predict foreign travel? We ought to put her on commission."

"I didn't let her look at my hand," Emily admitted.

"Don't blame you! She told my friend Jackie Churchill there was gonna be a drowning this weekend. Can you imagine it? Jacks was all set to enjoy her hen night and then she said that. Put a right downer on the weekend 'til we saw the trick. You see it? The magician walking on water?"

"Yes. You know, when he disappeared, I thought he must have drowned."

"Me and all. We was up in the big wheel with Jackie."

"I talked to her afterwards. With her friend in the blue—Chantal? One of her bridesmaids."

"That's it. We saw the magician walk on the water, with his feet just skimming on top of the waves. Then he vanished. Gave me a right scare, after what *she* said. Then he flew up in the air. Honest! You can laugh but I dunno how else to describe it. He flew up to that fish place, Poison, and we saw him by the window, waving. He was sort of hovering there, all lit up. Like an angel? Do you know how they done it?"

"You know when you're at a bus stop late at night—one of those covered stops with plastic seats and glass panels, and an electronic display telling you when the next bus is due?"

"He was on top of a bus? They drove a bus into the sea?" Dawn was impressed.

"No. I'm talking about the display, when it's dark it's kind of . . . it's reflected back and forth between the two glass panels and then it's projected *beyond* them."

"We don't have displays on bus stops in Torquay. You'd be lucky to get a cover on a bus stop, to be honest. Maybe it's different in London. But if you live in the countryside, if you haven't passed your driving test—or you've got disqualified, or you're too old to drive, or too young—you can expect to get cold and wet waiting to get wherever you're going."

"Well, the display, it's like a hologram. The illusion's called a Pepper's Ghost."

Dawn shook her head at the foolishness of such a notion. "Nope! I've talked to my brother about it. We're thinking sunken rope bridge." She typed on her keyboard to bring up some flight details and looked at the screen in front of her. "You'd go from London, yeah? So to get to Rio, you'd fly from Heathrow. One stopover, it'd be about six hundred and fifty quid. Costs you more to go direct.

Depends what time of year. You want to avoid the school holidays to get the best deal."

Emily made a few notes in her notebook. "Thanks, I'll think about it. The ticket wasn't for her, was it? Madame Nova? Wasn't it for a friend? I think he flew out yesterday."

"Yeah. Something to do with the Olympics—he was only gonna be there for the weekend. He's back Monday. I'd want to stay for longer if it was me. Can I say something?"

"Yes."

"Whoever done that to your face, he's not worth it."

"Thanks. It was . . . I tripped and fell."

"Course you did." Dawn picked up one of Fly Me to the Moon's business cards from a saucer by her desk and held it out to Emily.

Emily took it and walked to the door of the shop.

"You take care of yourself," said Dawn. And she meant it.

CHAPTER NINETEEN
A PSYCHIC WITH A NOOSE

When Emily got back to the hotel, she waited outside the Ballroom and intercepted Dr. Muriel as she came out for lunch.

"How's Edmund's paranormal challenge going?"

Dr. Muriel made a face. "I rather suspect the reason everyone's been sworn to secrecy is because it's so boring. If word got out, it would ruin Edmund's reputation." She smiled her most mischievous smile. "Oh, don't take my word for it. You *must* come in after the break and see for yourself."

Emily updated Dr. Muriel on her discovery at the Fly Me to the Moon Travel Agency.

"Clever you. So Madame Nova got rid of Edmund's technical advisor by buying him a ticket to Brazil. But does it follow that she was also responsible for Peg's death, and maybe Trina's, and the attack on you? If so, why?"

"I don't know. She'd have to be working with someone else, I think."

"With the other chap out of the way, it gave Chris the chance to get down here. Could she be working with him?"

No, Emily trusted Chris.

Dr. Muriel seemed relieved. She liked him, too. "If it's one of the psychic people who's making a bid for Edmund's money—trying to intimidate him, perhaps—it's too bad they didn't realize they could just turn up in the Ballroom and bore him to death."

Emily laughed. "Could be someone she knows from Torquay."

"Interesting. That obscene drawing in the Winston Churchill

room must have been done by a local youth, don't you think? Typical antiauthoritarian gesture from someone who feels disenfranchised. Must mean that people other than conference delegates have found their way in to the hotel. Everybody and his dog could have got in through the main entrance last night after Madame Nova's performance in front of the steps—it was impossible for the night porter to check everyone's pass as we all came back in."

But Emily had a good idea who had been responsible for the drawing in the Winston Churchill room. And it wasn't a local youth. "I think that may have been Trina's handiwork."

"Ah. Well. I think you're probably right—a crude commentary on the patriarchal society that served her so ill. Poor Trina. Never mind. With the ticket to Rio, you have a piece of evidence tying Madame Nova to Edmund, if not to Peg and Trina." Dr. Muriel began to walk toward the Riviera Lounge. "They've got a buffet set up over there. Coming?"

"I'll see you there in a minute. I want to go down to the pool to the place where I was attacked, to see if there's a way in from outside."

"Keep your eyes open for a psychic with a noose," called Dr. Muriel, loud enough for a few people to turn round, slightly alarmed, wondering if she was making a public announcement. When they saw her striding toward a table laden with cold meat pies, pickles, salads, quiches and cheese, with big glass bowls of sherry trifle for after, some ignored her and turned back to what they were doing, but many got up and followed her, as if she was the Pied Piper and they were Hamelin's enchanted children.

◆　◆　◆

When she reached the spa, Emily stood and looked at the pool. The conference was now underway, so no one was using it to swim, though there was a very hairy man in the Jacuzzi. The spa was in the basement of the hotel, but the ground level at the front was lower than it was at the back of the hotel, where the main entrance was situated. Through the windows at the other side of the pool, Emily could see a sunken, landscaped garden with an ornamental pond, and a winding, wheelchair-friendly path leading up to the main road. At the other side of that, though it was not visible from the pool, there was the beach. Could someone have got in from the garden last night and banged her over the head, or could it only have been a hotel guest or an employee who attacked her? And what had Bobby Blue Suit been doing down here in the middle of the night?

Emily walked past the pool toward the door leading out to the garden. It was cool and dark here, out of sight of the pool. She heard a rhythmic tap-tapping on the floor, the sound getting closer. She knew what it was—dogs' paws on marble. Behind her, Bobby Blue Suit was advancing with his dachshunds, the dogs' three short leads hooked onto one thin, blue leather strap that he held between his two hands, snapping it taut, his knuckles white with the effort.

A psychic with a noose!

Three thoughts occurred to her simultaneously: Bobby might have pretended to find her last night when he was really attacking her. A thin, leather dog's lead would make an efficient garrote. Bobby was harmless.

Emily opened her handbag and found the bags of dog treats she had bought for Shirley, Eddie and Elvis. Eddie seemed particularly pleased to see her, perhaps hoping for another taste of her blood.

Emily passed the treats to Bobby. "I think someone hit me over the head last night. Did you see anyone when you were walking the dogs?"

Bobby shook his head. "What's the world coming to that you're not safe in a hotel in Devon? Just glad we could be there for you, girl."

"Why were you down here last night, anyway? Wouldn't it be easier to go in and out of the main entrance?"

"You can use your room key to unlock a little door that goes out into the garden at the front there. It stops outsiders getting in but it means hotel guests can pass in and out without bothering the staff. If I go out of the main entrance after hours, I've got to get the night porter to let me out and then let me back in again, and if he's off on his rounds, I've got to ring a bell to find him. But if I come in and out this way, I can be self-sufficient. I can come straight down from my room in the elevator and go back up the same way. Right, we'd better go upstairs."

"Going up to face Edmund?"

"We've done that, Emily."

No need to ask how it had gone, then. Emily looked at Bobby in his shabby suit. It occurred to her that someone using the name Bobby Blue Suit wouldn't have to go to the expense of finding something different to wear every time he made an appearance on stage. Poor Bobby. He needed Edmund's money. But he hadn't won it.

CHAPTER TWENTY

AGATHA CHRISTIE'S HOUSE

Emily and Bobby helped themselves to lunch in the Riviera Lounge and went to join Dr. Muriel, who was with people who—if not quite old friends—at least felt familiar, even though she'd met them only the day before, or the day before that: Gerald, Edmund and Joseph Seppardi (though Joseph was sitting a little apart from the others, as always).

Looking around at other tables, Emily realized she was also starting to recognize people among the delegates whose names and faces, up till now, had been one big blur. There was Miriam Starling— *Hop, hop!*—and with her the German professors, Marta and Birgitte. Philip who fancied himself as Fred Astaire. Cheese-faced Ian. Romeo with his long, black curls and red neckerchief, looking as if he was auditioning to be a character in a D. H. Lawrence book. The psychic women with pixie haircuts and silver rings who had joined Peg's positivity circle.

The preoccupation of all these people with the main business of the conference seemed to highlight their innocence and set them apart from what had happened to Trina and Peg. They were intent on debate, not murder. Wasn't violence the last resort of people who couldn't make themselves understood, who couldn't get their way by persuasion?

"Ah. Interesting," said Dr. Muriel when Emily suggested it. But then, she often said that.

"He's gone!" Sarah said, running into the Riviera Lounge.

"Who?" said Joseph Seppardi.

"Tim! We went to Agatha Christie's house and he's gone missing."

"From the boat?" said Gerald. "Did he go overboard?"

Not another drowning!

"No. We went on a vintage bus. He went missing once we got to the house. One minute he was there, right next to me. The next minute . . . I've searched high and low. Joe, can you help?"

Joseph Seppardi sat quite still, his hands resting on his long legs. "Sarah . . ."

Bobby Blue Suit said, "Shirley gets a very strong feel for location. Abductions, missing persons. I can help, if you'll just give me something that belongs to him."

"Joe, please!" Sarah ignored Bobby. "I know you can do it."

"Sarah, I can see you want to help people. This isn't the way to do it."

"You leave this to me," said Bobby. "I know how to handle it." He knelt and petted his dogs. "Come on, Shirley, come on, girl. We've got to find this man. Elvis, Eddie, you send the word out. A man's in trouble. Tell the ghost dogs. They can help us find him."

Shirley stood and wagged her tail. Elvis and Eddie got to their feet and wagged their tails, too. Bobby reached into his pocket and gave each of them one of the treats Emily had bought that morning. They yipped.

"It's all right," said Sarah. "Joe can do it. Joe, he's trapped somewhere. Down a ditch or something. You can find him. I know you can do it. I've seen what you can do. Why won't you let other people see it? Then you could help more of them."

Bobby appealed to Gerald and Dr. Muriel. "The police won't admit it, but they do rely on help in cases like this from psychics like myself."

Sarah said, "Let Joseph do it. Please."

Joseph took out his phone and dialed a number. No answer. He punched in a short text message and sent it.

Bobby's dachshunds started barking. Bobby was energized. "I can feel him. He's near. Tim's alive. Tell me where to find him, Shirley."

Sarah's phone started ringing.

"We have to go back into the Ballroom," said Edmund. "But I have a feeling Tim's going to be OK."

He strode off. Gerald and Dr. Muriel followed him, Dr. Muriel beckoning for Emily to join them.

As Emily walked toward the Ballroom, she heard Sarah answer her phone. "Tim! Thank goodness." Her voice was self-conscious, a little too loud. "A ditch? Yes. Well, I'm glad you're out now. If you make your way back to the hotel, I'll meet you here . . ." She spoke more quietly, but Emily could still hear her. "No, he wouldn't. He said he didn't want to . . . I know. I know. I know . . . I'm sure you did. I know. I'm sorry."

When Emily looked back, Bobby raised his eyebrows at her, bemused by this amateurish attempt at fakery.

Edmund sighed as he held the door of the Ballroom open for Emily. "After you."

CHAPTER TWENTY-ONE
A MESSAGE FROM PEG

Emily went into the Ballroom, thinking she would find a chair and sit discreetly at the back. But Edmund, Gerald and Dr. Muriel insisted that she join them at the front, under a curtain-swagged bay window, where they sat in a line on hard-backed chairs, looking uncomfortable—the chauffeur, the cook and the butler invited to enjoy themselves at the staff Christmas party upstairs at the big house. Fortunately no one asked them to dance.

"Why have you got such a big room when you're seeing one person at a time?" Emily asked.

"They like to walk around, some of them," said Edmund. "And it helps us see the space around them, to be honest, in case they try any tricks. Who's next, Gerald? What's it say on the sheet?"

"Chap called Ian Wallender."

"Is that the one with a face like a Stilton cheese?" Emily asked.

Gerald nodded. "That's the one."

"I thought he was an astronomer."

"Astrologer," said Dr. Muriel. "My mistake."

Ian came into the room and introduced himself. He made good use of the space as he prepared, walking around, whispering to himself, gesturing. Finally, he came and stood in front of Edmund.

"I have a woman here named Margaret." Ian spoke softly. "Goes by Peg or Peggy."

"Here we go!" said Edmund to Gerald.

Dr. Muriel made a face that suggested this wasn't the first time they'd had a visit from someone called Peg that day.

Ian burbled on for about twenty minutes with nonspecific details about Peg's life, her devotion to her family, her love of paisley scarves.

"Does she have a message for us?" enquired Edmund pleasantly.

Ian considered this. He paced. He came to a stop in front of Edmund again. "Yes. She says, 'Don't worry, dears. I didn't feel any pain at the end.'"

"That's interesting," said Edmund. "That's very interesting, thank you." His tone was more polite than Emily had expected it to be.

Ian relaxed. He looked pleased.

"I'm sure you understand our position," said Edmund. "Information like this is difficult to verify. Or, if it's not difficult to verify, then that's because it's in the public domain and easily obtainable. It's very hard for us to determine if you've made some kind of paranormal connection with this lady, who reminds me—I can't speak for my colleagues, of course—but she reminds me very much of someone we knew who died recently, who we cared about. She was called Peg."

Ian was wary now, not sure if he'd won the challenge or if Edmund was making fun of him.

But Edmund maintained his polite tone. "I have devised a question that will help to ensure fairness for everyone who undertakes this challenge. Gerald here—the president, as I'm sure you know, of the Royal Society for the Exploration of Science and Culture—Gerald will help me determine whether or not we've made contact with someone in the spirit world."

Gerald smiled and nodded graciously.

Edmund said, "I will ask the same question, under the same circumstances, of everyone who takes part. That's why we asked you to sign a confidentiality agreement before you arrived, Ian. Are you prepared to abide by it? If you break our confidence, I'm afraid I'll have no choice but to inform the professional organization who represents you. They'll terminate your membership immediately. You understand?"

Ian nodded, intrigued, but still wary. Emily was also intrigued, and quite excited. But then, she hadn't had to sit through the same spiel a dozen times.

Edmund said, "We'd like you to make contact with Lady Lacey Carmichael, a past president of the society. And before you give me a lot of generic stuff about her likes and dislikes, let me explain what we need you to do. She promised to try to make contact after she died, if she could. To guard against any . . . misunderstanding, she left a password that she would use, if she ever got through. Understand?"

Ian nodded.

"No one knows it except the president of the society."

"It has never been revealed to anyone else," said Gerald.

"So. Can you let me have the password, please?"

Ian tried. He tried and tried. But he couldn't do it.

♦　♦　♦

"That was the last one," said Gerald, when Ian had left the room. "There's a cream tea set up in the Riviera Lounge for all the ravenous delegates. Shall we join them?"

"I won't, if you don't mind," said Edmund. "I'm going up to my room. I've got some work to do."

It was the last they saw of him. Later that afternoon, as the sun set on the horizon, Edmund Zenon walked into the sea. He didn't come back again.

CHAPTER TWENTY-TWO
NOT MUCH OF A TRICK

The scones were freshly made and buttery, still warm from the oven, piled up on blue pottery platters the size of tractor wheels. There were dishes of strawberry jam and clotted cream laid out next to the platters, to accompany the scones—the only question being whether to put the jam on first, or the cream. It was a question that Emily had heard fiercely debated whenever a cream tea was served to two or more people in England, and one that she was certain would never be resolved, even if the Queen were to issue a royal proclamation.

There were cucumber sandwiches and miniature salmon tartlets for those who were too hungry to be satisfied by scones, cream and jam. There was plenty of strong, milky tea to wash it all down. The feast had been set out on a long buffet table by the window overlooking the sea. The usual mix of anthropologists, zoologists, ethicists, philosophers, theologians, spiritualists, astronomers, astrologers and psychics crowded around the buffet table, chattering appreciatively about the sessions they had just attended at the Belief and Beyond conference as they piled up their plates, some veterans observing a one-for-the-plate, one-for-the-mouth rule that ensured their blood sugar wouldn't dip too low before the next meal.

It was around five thirty and the sky was already dark; the sea a flat, glistening gray, like roof slates after a downpour. Emily, Dr. Muriel and Gerald edged their way in and helped themselves to food and tea. They were well placed to see what happened next.

"Is that the magician?" someone said. A finger pointed out the window to where a fairy path of flat rocks stuck out above the waves, like an improvised jetty going from the beach into the sea. This was just beneath the hotel, about a mile away from where the magician had performed his trick last night. Most people couldn't see anything. Many were happy to explain to the people who claimed to see something *why* they couldn't be seeing Edmund Zenon.

"He's up in his room."

"There's no one there."

"It's a trick of the light."

But there was someone—something—there, a black flapping thing whose form was picked out intermittently by the moon rising in the sky, whenever the clouds drifted away.

"It is the magician!"

People were surer of it now. "There's his top hat and cape."

The audience was glad to be standing by the big picture window looking down on the magician below. The view was like being in the front row of the dress circle of a theater. It was clearer from up here than it would have been from the beach. Also, it was warmer.

The trick was different than it had been the night before. There were no excited crowds, just the slow progression of the figure in the cape over slippery rocks. But the not-quite-there glimpses of the performance were similar. The arms outstretched; the top hat and cape; the flickering, faltering light. Emily wondered if this was a performance or a rehearsal . . . or whether it mattered to Edmund, so long as people talked about it afterwards. If the magician vanished again and reappeared, where would he turn up? The Riviera Lounge was the obvious place.

The magician kept walking. The sea had been flat but now the wind changed and the waves got choppier than they had been the night before. His cape swirled around him. But he kept walking. At the edge of the last stone visible above the sea, he hesitated for a moment. Then he stepped forward. But instead of walking on top of the water, he seemed to be submerged, almost immediately. The top hat floated off on the waves. The cape, above him, also floated on the water. No sign of the magician. But then, the disappearance, the suggestion that he might actually have drowned, this was part of the illusion, right?

In the Riviera Lounge, those who had watched the walking-on-water trick the night before provided a commentary for those who hadn't. Those who hadn't seen the trick but had heard about it also chimed in. Finally, those who were watching it—not to be left out—explained what was happening now to the people around them who were also watching.

Soon there were murmurs of alarm.

"He hasn't come back up. Where is he? Is he there?"

"Has he drowned?"

"He hasn't drowned. It's all part of it."

"Not much of a trick."

"I prefer close-up magic."

"I told you about that Glaswegian at the Soho Theatre in London? Best close-up magic I ever saw, if you could put up with the swearing."

"I do like Penn and Teller."

"David Copperfield."

"Are you sure he hasn't drowned?"

"It's all part of it. He'll show up here in a minute. Or at a pub in town."

"Ah, now that's an idea. Do you fancy a drink before dinner?"

They were bored with it. Nothing much was happening. Their work was more interesting to them. They munched their cucumber sandwiches and nibbled their scones, and they resumed talking about the conference and the day's sessions, and what they could expect to hear tomorrow.

"It wasn't very polished, was it?" said Gerald, disappointed.

"Do you think something went wrong?" asked Emily. "Should I call someone?"

"Call Edmund," said Dr. Muriel.

Gerald called Edmund's mobile phone but it went straight to voicemail, so Emily and Dr. Muriel went to Reception to ask Mandy Miller to call his room. But Mandy wouldn't do it. Edmund had left strict instructions that he wasn't to be disturbed.

Emily and Dr. Muriel knew which room he was in: number thirty-six, the room that should rightfully have been Dr. Muriel's. They took the stairs to get there.

When they reached his room, they knocked. There was no answer.

"Should we try and knock it down?" Emily shrugged her shoulders a few times to loosen them, preparing for impact.

"I always suggest to my undergraduates they should find the easiest way to tackle a problem and start with that." Dr. Muriel turned the handle and the door opened. "Not that they listen. Nobody signs up for a philosophy course because they like the simple things in life. If you ever want a change of career, Emily, do let me know."

They went in. The room was neat and tidy. And empty. Dr. Muriel paused to take a quick, regretful look at the French windows that led onto a balcony overlooking the sea, then they went together to the bathroom and opened the door, very slowly. It was empty. Edmund's toothpaste, toothbrush, deodorant and shaving accessories were lined up neatly on the bathroom shelf. An attractive claw-footed Victorian bath stood in the middle of the room. Mercifully, Edmund was not in it.

"Why did he go down to those rocks and walk into the sea?" asked Dr. Muriel.

"Or, put it another way. Why hasn't he turned up again? I need to find Chris. If it's another trick, even a rehearsal, he'll know what's going on."

"At least we know one thing," said Dr. Muriel. "We know how the killer got into Peg's room."

"How?"

"The same way anyone gets in. By turning the handle."

"But Peg was inside the room. She'd have had the door locked."

"Well then, the killer would have got her to open it by knocking on it."

"You know, in my dream last night I heard someone knocking."

"Well, there you are, then. Just as well you didn't answer. Next thing you know, you'd have climbed fully clothed into the bath. Just like Peg."

The bath in Edmund's room was a large, Victorian steel bath standing on decorative steel claw feet in the middle of the room, just like the bath in Peg's room. The pipes for the taps and the wastewater were hidden under the floorboards. At one end of the bathroom there was a sink and a shelf for toiletries. There was a toilet and a walk-in shower at the other end of the room. A white wicker chair completed the look, so the hotel guests could throw discarded clothes or a bathrobe on it before stepping into the shower or the bath. Edmund's bathrobe was draped over the chair now. The bath itself was a couple of feet from each of the four walls. It was the kind of bathroom you'd promise yourself you'd have when you'd made a bit of money and moved to your dream home, if you didn't have one already.

Emily said, "If we knew what happened to Peg, maybe we could work out what happened to Edmund."

Dr. Muriel climbed, fully clothed, into the bath. "You're right. You need to try to kill me."

Emily looked around for something to choke her friend with. She took the belt from Edmund's toweling bathrobe. "You need to not struggle, because we know Peg didn't struggle or fight. We'll work out why in a minute." She looped the belt in her hands and came to stand behind Dr. Muriel. "The method of choking seems quite straightforward. The killer stands behind her with a belt or a pair of tights or something like that, and loops it round her neck, and before Peg realizes what's happening, the killer starts to choke her." Emily demonstrated, putting the belt around Dr. Muriel's neck.

"But that's it exactly! That's how it was done."

"How d'you mean?"

"The killer was pretending to demonstrate to Peg how Trina had been murdered. First, the knock at the door. Peg looks through the spyhole. It's someone she recognizes; she lets them in. This person has a theory about how Trina might have been murdered. The bath was similar to this one, wasn't it? They reenact it, with Peg standing in for Trina."

"Very clever. But who was it?"

"That we don't know. Your notebook, Emily, or your clever brain, will tell us the answer, I'm sure." Dr. Muriel got out of the bath. "I'm going to tell Gerald to call the police and ask them to look for Edmund. If anyone other than Gerald contacts them, they may think it's a hoax or a trick after yesterday's performance by the pier."

"I'll go and find Chris."

Chapter Twenty-Three
RECONCILIATION

Madame Nova was sitting in the lobby with Hilary as Emily passed through it looking for Chris. *She was sitting with Hilary.* It was a minor surprise, considering all the other things that had happened in the past two days.

Hilary had one hand on the handle of Madame Nova's wheelchair, proprietorially. There was a bottle of Merlot and a pint of orange juice and lemonade on the table next to them. Madame Nova held a half-empty wine glass.

Emily went over there. "You've heard about Edmund?"

Madame Nova's lips were stained a dark, inky blue from the wine. "Yes. Would you like a drink? Come and have a drink with us."

"You two know each other?" Emily asked her.

"Hilary's offered to share her room with me tonight. The hotel staff moved her, of course. So she doesn't have to stay where . . ." *Where Trina died.* Madame Nova didn't have to say it. She still hadn't answered Emily's question, though.

Hilary smiled. "Hotels always say they're fully booked, but when they need to, they can always find you a room, can't they?"

"But you two knew each other before?" Emily asked again.

Hilary ignored her. Madame Nova took so long to answer that Emily began to wonder if she'd heard the question. But even if her sunglasses were restricting her vision, Madame Nova's hearing should have been unaffected.

"I used to live in London," she said at last. "I had been a moderately successful stage actress. But after my daughter died, I couldn't work. I couldn't learn my lines. I got stage fright and couldn't go on one night. They were perfectly nice about it. But I couldn't go on the next night, or the night after that, or the night after." She took a sip of wine. "It was over for me. I packed up and moved down here. I have my shop. I amuse myself telling fortunes for tourists. Madame Nova." She took another sip of wine. "I should go by Madame Merlot. Wish I'd thought of that when I moved down here." She pulled the corners of her mouth down, to show she was making a joke against herself. She still hadn't answered Emily's question.

"We're sisters," said Hilary. She waited while Emily took that in. "After Vivienne's daughter died, we were estranged."

Madame Nova didn't say anything. Her bottle of wine was empty. She took another from a pocket in her leopard-skin cloak, and a corkscrew from a pocket on the other side. She clasped the bottle between her knees, withdrew the cork and poured herself a glass. In those quick, efficient movements—in the pursuit of more alcohol—she was determined and strong. Replacing the corkscrew in her pocket, she became frail again.

Hilary was determined and strong. She held herself upright, like a dancer. Like an ex-actress? She wore no makeup. Madame Nova was frail, heavily made-up, dressed in flamboyant clothes. They were so different. Then Madame Nova took off her sunglasses. She had a defeated look and Hilary seemed . . . exultant. But Emily saw a resemblance in their eyes—in the muddy-green color, at least, with the feathery flecks of brown in the green. She saw they could be sisters.

Hilary said to Madame Nova, "What's happened will bring us together. Both of us have suffered the death of a child."

That seemed a bit of a stretch, considering Trina was a runaway Hilary had picked up in London three days ago. But why not, if it was common ground they were after?

"Her garments, heavy with their drink," said Madame Nova, "pull'd the poor wretch from her melodious lay to muddy death." She took another sip of wine.

"Shouldn't it be 'bubbly death' rather than 'muddy death,' if you mean Trina?"

"You can't paraphrase Shakespeare," said Madame Nova.

"Ophelia," Hilary explained. "Vivienne was a very good Ophelia."

"Were you ever on stage, Hilary?"

"Only in the ensemble. I've had a few false starts over the years, trying to find what to do with myself."

At this, Madame Nova made a *tell me about it* face and took another drink.

"This is my best role—taking care of other people. I'm going to take care of Vivienne. She needs me. I truly believe this is why I was brought here. It was meant to be."

Madame Nova drained her glass and reached for the bottle. "People are always telling you how to make things better. They don't stop to consider whether you might like things the way they are. Not everyone wants to be sunny and friendly all the time."

Emily was a sunny and friendly person, usually. But she was glad Hilary hadn't taken it into her head to take care of *her*. She went off to find Chris.

◆　◆　◆

She found him in the Lamb and Dragon pub on the High Street with the Colonel and Tim, taking advantage of a pie and a pint deal offered by the landlord, with more pints consumed than pies.

Emily told them what she'd seen from the windows of the Riviera Lounge.

"It can't have been Ed walking into the sea," said Chris. "First of all, it's me that goes into the sea in that trick. He's the one who magically reappears moments later, dry as a bone, while I hide under the jetty. But that's not the point. We didn't have anything scheduled for tonight."

"Was there anything that would have made him want to take his own life?" Emily asked.

"Come on, Emily. You know Ed. He'd never do something like that."

"Well now," said the Colonel, quietly. "She said she'd get him to walk into the sea and he did."

"No way!" said Chris. "No way."

"I'll see you back at the hotel," Emily told them. "I just wanted to let you know about Edmund."

The three men raised their glasses in drinking-up gestures, to show that they would finish their pints and join her.

As she left the Lamb and Dragon, Emily had the sense of being watched. There! Over on the other side of the street, close enough to keep an eye on the door to the pub, but far enough away that he wouldn't be noticed unless you were looking for him; as embarrassed and superfluous as a man waiting for his wife to try on a dress in a department store changing room: Joseph Seppardi.

Emily crossed the street to tell him what had happened.

"Have you told Sarah?" he asked her.

Emily hadn't. She hadn't seen her since the earlier Tim-in-a-ditch nonsense.

"I can't watch both of them. I thought she'd be safe with that fortune-teller. The one who drinks too much." Joseph began to walk quickly, away from the pub. If he wanted to go back to the hotel, he was going in the wrong direction. He had long legs. Emily scampered to keep up with him. "She's vulnerable," he said. "They're both vulnerable. People prey on them. You know why the Colonel's called the Colonel?"

"No." Emily was getting slightly breathless. Where were they going?

"You ask him next time you see him. Put it this way: I wouldn't want him in charge of the search and rescue mission."

They stopped in front of A Little of What You Fancy. The shop was in darkness but there was a light on in the back, coming from the storeroom.

Joseph stood by the door to the shop, his long face miserable in the shadows. Emily shivered. It wasn't a crime to have a miserable face—though you'd never know it if you had ever tried to get on a country bus with one, as Emily had when she was a teenager, because country bus drivers like to say "cheer up" to anyone who isn't beaming with joy at stepping aboard their vehicle. (London bus drivers, of course, try to ignore their passengers altogether.) And there was nothing wrong with having a long face, either—otherwise why would people be so fond of horses? No, Emily decided. It was his otherworldliness that bothered her. She found him creepy.

"Are we looking for Sarah?" Emily whispered.

Joseph held his hand up. No answer.

Emily started to feel alarmed. "What's happened? What have you done with her?"

Still no answer. Joseph opened the door and went into the shop. Emily followed him. The novelty items Madame Nova stocked—the sparkly wings and the wands, the wigs, even the moustaches—were transformed in the shadows into treasures plundered from a fairy kingdom, kept out of sight in a dilapidated museum by an eccentric custodian. The darkness gave life to the things in the shop, rather than taking it away, as it did in fairy tales. On a shelf at head-height, Emily passed a giant rat with wary eyes. Like the rat bought as a prop by the professor from Hamelin, this one was made of gray fun fur. The wary eyes were plastic. But it seemed to breathe as the light from outside flickered along its length. Emily shuddered and moved on.

As she approached the storeroom through the darkened shop, Emily tried to prepare herself for something unpleasant. In the past twenty-four hours she had seen two women dead in their bath. She hoped she wouldn't see anything as awful as that, but she wanted to be ready, just in case. The sight she saw now was unexpected, though it was not unpleasant. It was Sarah, in the storeroom, in a towering wig.

She was sitting on a low stool in her ordinary clothes. The wig she wore was bright yellow and looked to be about two foot tall. There was a cuckoo clock in the front panel. Though Joseph Seppardi was as surprised as Emily by her appearance, Sarah didn't seem surprised to see either of them. She turned very, very slowly in their direction, keeping her neck stiff, opening her eyes wide and wrinkling her forehead, deploying the tiny little muscles under her scalp to keep the wig in place.

"Edmund's gone into the water," Emily said. "We don't think he's coming back."

Sarah thought about this for a moment. "There was one time I washed Liam's favorite cuddly toy in the washing machine when he was a toddler. It was filthy dirty and sticky and that. It came out clean and fluffy. You think they'll be pleased. But when you hand it over, they cry, because it smells different. I don't know how much of his senses Liam's got, wherever he is. I can't see or hear him. I need Joseph for that. But I don't want to risk him not recognizing me. I wouldn't want to go into the water to come out reborn, though Hilary told me I should do it."

"I don't think it was a baptism. Edmund had his stage clothes on. It might have been a trick that went wrong."

"You could say that about life, couldn't you? Put it on my headstone: 'It might have been a trick that went wrong.'"

Was *everyone* going to end up looking and sounding like a movie star? First Madame Nova in her sunglasses and flamboyant leopard-skin cloak. Now Sarah—sensible, ordinary, very nice Sarah—sitting here wearing a wig and wanting an aphorism on her headstone. Emily looked over at Joseph Seppardi, standing quietly in front of a display of comedy false teeth. His face was expressionless.

She turned back to Sarah. "Why are you wearing that wig, if you don't mind me asking?"

Sarah held up the keys to the shop. "Madame Nova said it would make me feel better. Said she comes into the back of her shop and tries on the wigs when she needs to cheer herself up."

Well, at least she hadn't suggested Sarah get herself a couple of bottles of Merlot. "Has it worked?"

Sarah smiled. "Yes, it has, a bit. You know, we came to Torquay because Liam said we should. And then he just went quiet on us when we got here."

Emily glanced over at Joseph again. No reaction.

"When Liam was a little boy, I used to say that if anything ever happened to him, I'd just walk out the door—not even shut it behind me—I'd just walk out the door and keep on walking until I reached the sea, and then I'd walk into it, and I'd still keep walking. I wouldn't care about anything. I wouldn't want to live. He was still a boy when he died, though he was old enough to have a job. I didn't walk out the door when I heard the news. When it came down to it, I didn't want to leave Tim. But sometimes I feel like I've walked through a door in my mind . . . like I've walked away from my sanity."

Emily looked at Sarah, sitting there in Madame Nova's wig, smiling vaguely. She spoke gently. "Well, if you didn't shut the door behind you, you can find your way back in."

CHAPTER TWENTY-FOUR
THE SÉANCE

Sarah removed the wig and stored it carefully in the back of Madame Nova's shop. She left with Emily and Joseph Seppardi, the three of them walking back to the hotel with the sound of the coastguards' helicopter overhead, its powerful light still searching the waves for signs of Edmund Zenon.

When they got back to the hotel, Dr. Muriel and Gerald were in the Riviera Lounge with Chris, the Colonel and Tim.

"Edmund's top hat and cape were found floating on the waves," Gerald told them. "But there's no sign of the man himself."

"We don't know that Edmund's dead," said Dr. Muriel, "so let's hold on to that. Perhaps he's hiding to see what people will say about him. It's another storytelling event?"

Chris smiled at her. The smile said, "No."

"There's an impromptu positivity circle going on in the Winston Churchill room, if anyone wants to join in," Gerald said. "Otherwise do join us for a drink here."

Emily didn't want a drink. She wanted to write up her notes. It would be noisy in the Riviera Lounge, so she decided to slip into the Winston Churchill room. The flip charts and conference paraphernalia had been moved to one side. A leaderless circle of women with pixie haircuts and silver rings sat disconsolately on blue velvet straight-backed chairs, trying to avert the outcome that had been determined for Edmund Zenon by fate or God or some human murderer. The women were humming, their eyes closed.

Emily sat at the side of the room. As she opened her notebook, she thought how empty it seemed without Peg. Peg and Edmund, in their different ways, had been charismatic figures. Had they been killed for their beliefs? If so, whoever was responsible was a miserable person if they preferred a world without interesting characters in it, so that only people with the same beliefs remained. But what beliefs would those be?

The notes Emily was making began to look like an obituary for Peg and Edmund. And what about Trina? No one could say she had been charismatic, though she had been memorable. Up there on the whiteboard, transformed into a star-bound rocket with a hashtag on it, Trina's antiauthoritarian graffiti served as a memorial of sorts.

The humming in the room had become a series of long, pulsing nasal sounds that were getting louder and more purposeful, as if the Winston Churchill room were an engine room for the universe, and the universe was a ship, and the noise alone could drive them all to a place where they could be useful. It seemed to Emily, as she closed her notebook and tiptoed off to the Riviera Lounge, that the need to be useful was a powerful motivator in most people.

"Emma!" It was Alice, the girl she and Dr. Muriel had met on the train on the way down to Torquay. "We've got your friend's forty pounds, me and Ben. For the ticket?"

"How did you get into the hotel? You're not staying here, are you?"

"I said Muriel was my auntie. That girl on reception let us in. Said she'd send security after us if we weren't back in five minutes."

We?

"I'm here with Ben. What's that humming all about, then? Those women in that room?"

"Edmund. He's gone missing."

"So it's true! We heard the helicopters. There's loads of rumors going round at the Lamb and Dragon."

Alice explained that, after getting into the hotel, she and Ben had split up to investigate. Alice had been drawn to the positivity circle by the sound of the humming, Ben had gone to the bar and the restaurant. Emily couldn't blame them for using the repayment of the debt as a cover for coming to the Hotel Majestic to try to find out what had happened to their hero. As for the sleuthing, well perhaps it came naturally to young British people? Emily almost felt proud.

When Emily and Alice got to the Riviera Lounge, they found Ben there with the others. Dr. Muriel had £40 stacked in front of her in £1 coins, silver coins and coppers. Ben was wearing his *I believe . . . in Edmund Zenon* T-shirt, recent events changing the ironic slogan into a naïvely hopeful statement. Gerald was checking his Twitter updates. The others were talking about having a séance.

"I didn't know the man," Joseph Seppardi was saying. "I mostly deal with bereaved family members. He has to want to talk to you. I'd rather not do it."

"You have to!" said Sarah. "He promised Chris last night he'd try to get through."

"That was a joke," said Chris.

"So what else are we going do, except sit here all night, waiting for news?" said Tim. "We may as well do something. I vote we go up to his room and see if Joe can contact him."

"I'm in," said Dr. Muriel. "I've a bottle of Scotch upstairs. I'll fetch it and meet you there."

"He's not really dead, though, is he?" said Alice. "This is part of it? This is part of the trick?"

"It doesn't look good," said Dr. Muriel.

"He'll come back," said Ben. He bit the inside of his mouth, the hollows under his cheekbones emphasizing the pallor of his gaunt face. "He has to. You know how he showed up in the Poisson d'Avril restaurant last time? Poisson d'Avril means April Fool. The first of April, that's Monday—Easter Monday. He'll come back again. I'm not . . . I know it sounds deluded. But it isn't. He'll come back. It's a code. A joke for his fans."

"That's an interesting way of looking at it," said Dr. Muriel kindly.

Derek the security guard appeared and beckoned to Alice and Ben. Time to leave. Emily couldn't see what harm they could do by staying, if Gerald's celebrity guest was dead. But Derek had his orders. He shepherded Alice and Ben from the hotel.

"How about it, Joseph?" said Tim when they had gone.

Joseph sighed. "I'd need something of Edmund's if I were to try to make contact."

"We could go up to his room," said Chris. "All his stuff's still lying around."

"You should ask someone else, if Joseph doesn't want to do it," said Gerald. "Give the man a break."

Sarah wouldn't hear of it. "All the best psychics have already had a go in the Ballroom today. All except Joseph. None of them passed the test. Joseph talks to our Liam. I know he does. Maybe that's why Liam brought us here. To get in touch with Edmund, find out what's happened." She seemed to have found her way back to normality—or her version of it—after the earlier wobble in A Little of What You Fancy. She had a mission, and it was the reason Liam had brought her here: to help Edmund's friends.

"I won't join you," said Gerald. He looked gray and tired. "I need to be up early tomorrow; the conference continues. I'll call you if there's any news."

◆   ◆   ◆

In Edmund's room, Tim put Joseph in the only armchair, positioned with his back to the French windows and balcony. Unsure which of Edmund's possessions would best help him to tune in to the man, Tim went around the room selecting things at random, piling Joseph's lap with a T-shirt, a pair of socks, a toothbrush, a comb and a copy of *Don't Believe the Hype*, so that he looked as though he'd just come back from an impulse-buying spree at a jumble sale.

Emily and Chris propped themselves up on the bed, as chaste as a courting couple in a Doris Day movie. Dr. Muriel was allocated the upright chair that went with the desk, and Tim and Sarah sat on pillows on the floor. Dr. Muriel had a sideways view of the windows. Chris and Emily looked directly at Joseph, and behind him the balcony—and beyond it the road to the town, and beyond that the sea, through the French windows. Out on the moonlit path that ran along the low sea wall, Emily could see Bobby Blue Suit with his dachshunds, walking down toward the town and then, once business was taken care of, turning around and heading back across the road to the hotel.

The whisky that Dr. Muriel had brought with her was a single malt from the Isle of Islay. It had a distinctive, peaty flavor. It was like drinking a bonfire; flames, then the taste of smoke. Everyone except Joseph had a tumbler of it, then they settled down to see what he could do.

He spoke solemnly. "I know that some of you don't believe in this. You don't have to believe. But you have to be prepared to listen, and Edmund—if he's out there—has to be prepared to come here to say something to you."

"It's our only chance to find out what's happened," said Sarah, breathlessly.

"Well," said Dr. Muriel, "Emily's very good at solving mysteries. And, of course, there's always the police."

"I need more time," Emily admitted.

"Shh," Sarah said. "Let's listen to Joseph."

Joseph put his hands together under his chin, resting his elbows on the armrests of his chair. "It may not be Edmund who comes here. He may send someone else . . . Let us prepare."

He told them they didn't have to join hands to create a circle. "This isn't a game of Ring a Ring o' Roses." But it seemed natural for Chris to take Emily's hand. Tim and Sarah held hands, too. It was quiet in the room for a long time. In the quiet and the darkness—there was only a small lamp on in the room, and outside, the full moon—it was like meditating. Everyone seemed to get lost in their thoughts.

"There's someone here," said Joseph.

Emily felt excited. Everyone sat up, waiting. You didn't have to believe in it to appreciate the theater of it. She felt Chris tense beside her, hoping it wouldn't be Edmund, because if it was someone else, Edmund might still be alive.

Joseph milked the pause like a judge in a television talent show.

"It's a lady," he continued, eventually. "She's showing me something. A . . . wedding gown. A beautiful white wedding gown with a long train, made of lace. And she's getting into a car. Lovely old thing. Looks like a Rolls-Royce. She's getting in the car with her husband. It must be her wedding day. Her brothers are there. Michael. Anyone know Michael?"

"Is it something to do with Peg?" Sarah asked.

Joseph thought not. Everyone else agreed.

Emily let go of Chris's hand and wrote down everything Joseph had said. Then her attention drifted to the path by the sea wall. She saw Sarah pushing Madame Nova up the hill in her wheelchair, wrapped up in her leopard-skin cloak, moving from the hotel toward the top of the cliffs, in the opposite direction from the town. No, not Sarah. Sarah was here in the room. It must be Hilary, doing her sisterly duty. Perhaps she put the same faith in the restorative properties of the sea air as Dr. Muriel and was using it to ward off Madame Nova's impending hangover.

The lady Joseph connected with had no news of Edmund Zenon.

"Do you have anything to tell us? Any message?" Sarah was disappointed. If Joseph didn't come up with something, Emily suspected she'd be off to Madame Nova's shop for another session with the wig tomorrow.

"There is something," said Joseph. "She's showing me. I don't hear it. One moment while I try to interpret it."

Emily looked around the room. Everyone was getting restless, even Tim. Only Sarah seemed convinced that Joseph might still prove he could connect with someone in the spirit world.

"I'm seeing . . . I'm seeing a big book, like an encyclopedia. I'm seeing tears. A sad face."

"Tears of a clown?" Chris suggested.

"No, it's . . . tragedy."

Ah. Very apt. Everyone nodded.

"And then I'm getting running around. Chasing."

"Benny Hill?" said Chris. "The comedian?"

"No. It's . . . I've got a big book, a sad face, running around or laughing or . . . Hold on. She's showing me a tombstone. A cemetery."

"I've got it!" said Dr. Muriel. She actually put her hand up. "I've never been to a séance before. It *is* like a game of charades! You're at Highgate Cemetery—in London. That's where Karl Marx is buried. The big book represents history. Then we had tragedy. Then we had farce. It's a quote of his. History repeats itself, first as tragedy, then as farce."

"Could be." No one looked convinced. It didn't seem relevant. Emily wrote it down anyway.

Joseph looked as if he'd just run the London Marathon. He was completely done in. "Yes, that's it. History repeats itself. First as tragedy, then as farce."

"That's the message?" said Chris. "It doesn't sound like Ed."

"I don't think it was Edmund," said Joseph Seppardi. "It was something the lady wanted me to pass on."

She had not long departed, and they were waiting for someone else to show, or for Joseph Seppardi to throw in the towel, when Emily noticed Madame Nova wheeling herself back across the road to the hotel. There was no sign of Hilary. Had they had a row? Emily knew that reconciliations could be difficult after long periods apart, but she hoped they hadn't fallen out again.

Chris was getting restless, clenching and unclenching his fists. She glanced at him and he relaxed his hands and smiled. When she looked back, Madame Nova had already disappeared.

Although all of them would have said, when they first went into the room, that it would be impossible to sleep, it now seemed a good idea to turn in for the night. Combined with the long meditative silences and the whisky, the séance had had a soporific effect on everyone but Chris—and Joseph Seppardi, who was so tired, he looked as though he'd be ready for his grave sooner than his bed. They agreed to meet for breakfast, unless there was any news.

Dr. Muriel turned her phone back on. But there had been no call from Gerald. Chris checked his phone, too. No news, good or bad.

Emily was halfway down the corridor when she heard Chris call her name. He took her hand and led her to a recess where a fire extinguisher was stored next to an antique vase on a decorative table. There was room for the two of them to stand while everyone else wandered off to their rooms. "Where are you going after this?"

It was late. What did he have in mind? A late-night clifftop stroll with a wheelchair? Or something more romantic?

"I mean after we leave here—after Torquay."

Emily was tired. Did they have to talk about it now? "I'm going back to London. Gerald's booked my ticket for tomorrow. I'm back to work on Tuesday."

"Ever fancy a life of adventure?"

Emily felt slightly defensive. Honestly, what was wrong with working in an office?

Chris smiled at her. "You know, I'd like to set up a traveling theater troupe, going from place to place, working with local actors, bringing entertainment to people who would really appreciate it. How's that sound?"

It did sound quite interesting. She'd need to sleep on it. She'd need to save up and rent out her flat and . . .

"I think you'd be good at it, Emily. I'd love to work with you."

"Could we talk about it tomorrow? I'm really tired."

"Course!" He gave her the sweetest smile; he seemed so pleased. "I was thinking maybe the first stop should be Kenya."

"Oh, Chris. No. I mean, I love zebras as much as the next person. No. I like my life in London."

"Not just zebras. There are lakes and mountains and the Indian Ocean; giraffes and leopards and wildebeest . . . lots of wildebeest. Just"—he shrugged, poor Trina—"no tigers."

Emily was so tired! "I don't have an opinion about wildebeest. I do like giraffes."

"I can't do the commercial stuff. I can't do London." He put his hand on her shoulder and closed his eyes. He leaned forward. Was he going to kiss her? Or fall asleep on her? She took a step back.

"Good night, Chris."

Emily went upstairs—alone—and dreamed a dreamless sleep. When she woke up, she knew who the murderer was.

CHAPTER TWENTY-FIVE
A BETTER PLACE

As they gathered in the restaurant for breakfast, Gerald told them the sad news. Edmund's body had been found washed up on the beach at dawn. It was too early to determine the cause of death; the body had sustained some battering from the rocks in the water.

Chris hugged Emily as if he was trying to comfort her. She could feel his heart beat and smell the soap he had washed with that morning.

Whatever the cause of Edmund's death, it was newsworthy. The press were outside: print journalists, radio news teams and broadcasters from network television.

"Poor Peg," said Gerald. "I can't help thinking she would have loved the press attention. We can only hope she finds some way—wherever she is—to ensure her positivity book is given as much coverage as Edmund's." He was trying to make light of it but his voice was choked. "I will just need to ask you to be cautious if you put anything on Twitter. Our recent updates will be raked over and used in articles about the tragedy." He had the Sunday newspapers in front of him. "Most of it's online, given that Edmund's body has only just been found. But we can expect longer pieces in both the broadsheets and the tabloids tomorrow."

At other tables beyond theirs, the conference participants continued with their preparations for the day. They knew that Edmund was missing and Peg had died—Trina's death, as it was the death of a young woman not directly connected to the conference, had been kept from most of them—and they were subdued, chatting quietly, respectful of the tragedy around them. But their lives moved at a normal pace.

The lives of those affected had slowed down to an underwater pace, everything distorted and surreal, words formed but not reaching the hearer, every breath just bubbles, nothing making sense. They were like marbles in a machine that had been constructed by a child for its entertainment, rattling along on their clockwise journey—and then suddenly spiraling counterclockwise in this particular part of it, while all the other marbles went clockwise. Sooner or later they'd be going clockwise again, unless they got caught in this bit of the machine and never progressed beyond it. It was difficult to know what would come next if you were only a marble and not the machine's maker.

Those Emily counted among the counterclockwise, underwater marble people were Tim and Sarah—sitting with the Colonel and Joseph Seppardi—and Gerald, Chris and Dr. Muriel, who were sitting with her.

"I wish we knew what happened to Edmund," said Sarah.

"Emily knows." Dr. Muriel looked over at her friend. "Don't you?"

Chris stretched his legs out and folded his arms, emphasizing how big and tall he was, like a cat preparing for a fight. "It isn't suicide? I can't believe it's suicide."

Emily took a moment to put her thoughts in order before she began to explain what she knew. "Everyone who saw the image of Edmund Zenon walking on water had a different reaction to it. Even if they didn't agree on what might happen, they all knew when it would take place, and where: Easter weekend. Torquay. From the moment those posters went up, Edmund's fate was sealed. Three people were murdered because of what that image suggested to one person who saw it."

"So it was someone in Torquay?" said Sarah.

"It wasn't just people in Torquay who saw it. The image was projected onto the Royal Festival Hall in London, right by the Thames, in the heart of the city. It was . . . well, if you were a person with deeply held religious convictions, who had an estranged sister living in Torquay, it would seem like a call to action. Especially if a person who had been a big part of your life in recent years had decided to leave you to go to Africa, and you were looking for guidance about what to do next."

"Hilary!" said Tim. "Where is Hilary?"

"I don't get it," Sarah said. "Where did Trina fit in?"

"Hilary practically fell over her in an underpass in Waterloo, right after she'd seen the image of Edmund on the Royal Festival Hall. She thought if she recruited Trina and used her as a stooge during the Pledge and Plunge sessions by the sea, she might encourage others to join in. She might revive the Colonel's spirits and encourage him to stay in England for another tour in the summer. I think that signs from God are just like any other signs—like messages from the spirit world, if you believe in them. You have to know how to interpret them. So Hilary picked up Trina and brought her to Torquay, not quite knowing what she was going to do when she got here, but thinking Trina was part of the plan. But when the Colonel decided he would still rather go to Africa, she became expendable. In fact, when the Colonel used Trina's education as a reason why Hilary should stay behind, Hilary decided to get rid of her."

"No!" said Sarah. "I can't believe it. Who would do something like that?"

"It's not as bad as it sounds, if you believe you're sending someone to a better place."

The Colonel stood up. "This is all wrong. You can't make these accusations while Hilary's not here to defend herself. I'll go and find her."

Chris stood up, ready to stop him leaving. "You mean you'll go and warn her."

"What about the predictions about drowning?" Gerald asked Emily. "You're not saying those originated with Hilary?"

"No. But the Colonel's right. We should go and fetch Hilary. And Madame Nova."

Tim pointed out of the window at the bay below them. "You won't get hold of Madame Nova. I had no idea she was keen on surfing. Chilly weather for it, mind. Jolly windy, too. It's a wonder that cloak's not flapping about all over the place."

They looked out of the window and there was Madame Nova, kneeling on a surfboard on the sea, leopard-skin cloak wrapped around her, hood up, using an oar to paddle herself out to deeper water. The assembled members of the press had also spotted her. Journalists, broadcasters and photographers stood on the path above the beach, recording and commenting on her progress.

"Maybe she's looking for Edmund?" said Gerald. He didn't sound convinced. "She might not know his body's been found. Anyone speak to her or Hilary this morning?"

"Something's up!" Tim exclaimed. "What has she done with Hilary?"

They ran out of the Riviera Lounge and up to the room the two women had shared temporarily, collecting Mandy Miller from Reception with her master key along the way; marbles rattling counterclockwise, bumping into each other and propelling themselves upwards, up the stairs, not knowing what they would find next, and whether it would make them feel like rolling all the way back down again.

"Whatever's happened, it can't be good," said Dr. Muriel, stick in hand, huffing up the stairs.

Chapter Twenty-Six
Ophelia

There was no sign of Hilary in the bedroom she had shared with Madame Nova the night before. The sheets on the twin beds were rumpled. Madame Nova's mohair coat was thrown carelessly over a chair. There were empty bottles of red wine and half-empty bottles of pills on the floor, and bangles and earrings and a jar of night cream on a bedside table.

Emily and Dr. Muriel exchanged a heavy look and went to the bathroom. Dr. Muriel used one end of her stick to push open the door. There was a pleasant, tumbling sound, like an artificial waterfall in an expensive Thai restaurant. It got louder as the door swung open.

There, in the bath, was Madame Nova, in a high-necked, long-sleeved white nightgown—borrowed from Sarah, presumably. She was lying in about an inch of water, with the taps still running.

Madame Nova! But wasn't she . . . ? Well, if *she* was here, then who was on the surfboard paddling out to sea? It took a few moments for everyone to try to make sense of this.

Chris got closer. "She's alive. She's pretty groggy, but she's still with us."

Emily turned the taps off. Chris and Gerald pulled Madame Nova from the bath in her nightgown. Dr. Muriel wrapped her in towels. Sarah steered her to the bedroom, instructing her to put one foot in front of the other and keep moving, and then they laid her on one of the beds.

"M'all right," said Madame Nova, eyes still closed, voice slurry. She had a bruise above her eye and a cut on her lip. "Juss leave me alone."

Mandy Miller dialed 999.

"Did Hilary do this to you?" Emily asked Madame Nova.

Madame Nova's hand went to her forehead, exploring the lump that had come up there. "Couldn't stay with me in Torquay. How could she? We had another falling out. S'OK, she's gone."

"Why did you fall out last time?" Sarah asked her.

"It was after her daughter died," Emily explained.

"Hilary didn't . . . she didn't kill your child?"

"Don't be so melodramatic!" Madame Nova said, eyes still closed, arms flung about, somewhat melodramatically. "Said she was in a better place, 's all. Insensitive. You know what it's like, Sarah. I couldn't cope with it."

Gerald went to the bedroom window. It was at the front of the hotel, overlooking the sea. "What on earth is she doing out there? I presume that's Hilary. Is she making her escape? I mean, where would she hope to get to? Next stop's France, isn't it?"

"She might make it to Guernsey," said Dr. Muriel, joining him. "Oh, hold on. She appears to have stopped."

They all went to the window. The coastguard's boat had been launched from the harbor and was now *wump-wumphing* over the waves in Hilary's direction. She was crouched on the surfboard, facing the hotel.

Emily said, "It was Hilary who walked into the water last night, dressed in Edmund's stage clothes."

The group at the window turned to look at Emily as they made sense of that.

"No!" said Sarah.

"Of course!" said Dr. Muriel. "How clever."

"She stole the top hat and cape from the bar on Friday night—they were lying about because people had borrowed them to dress up in them. Remember Philip, pretending to be Fred Astaire?"

"I do," admitted Dr. Muriel.

"When Hilary walked into the water last night, she relied on people only glimpsing what was happening, and making assumptions about what they were seeing, filling in the gaps if necessary."

Gerald nodded. "We thought it was Edmund, of course, because of the trick by the pier."

"She did a one-woman, low-tech version of that trick: slipping into the water, shedding the top hat and cape, and then creeping back to the hotel across the road, coming in through the door by the swimming pool."

Dr. Muriel had enjoyed her morning swim every day at the hotel. "There's nothing odd about someone coming back from the spa with wet hair," she said. "So no one would suspect her if they saw her once she got inside."

"And outside," Emily said, "if anyone was paying attention, they were looking for a magician, not a middle-aged woman in ordinary clothes. She borrowed Edmund's reverse-disguise thinking for that, too."

"But where was Edmund?" said Tim.

"She had already killed him."

"No!" said Sarah. It was her default reaction.

Emily suspected Sarah didn't yet want to believe that Edmund had died, whether in the water or elsewhere. "I don't know this, I'm guessing, but I think Hilary went up to his room and presented her hypothesis, the way she did with Peg, showing how someone could sneak up with a garrote . . . and then she choked him. Or maybe she drugged him or hit him over the head with something heavy. Anyway, she killed him and put him in the wheelchair, and she dressed him up in Madame Nova's hooded leopard-skin cloak and sunglasses. He'd be too difficult to move once rigor mortis started to set in, but she's a strong woman—she ought to have been able to get him into the chair while he was still warm. Then she wheeled him to her room and left him there while she dressed up in his stage clothes, went down in the elevator, and then walked out on the rocks and into the sea, pretending to be him."

"But why?" asked Dr. Muriel. That was her default question.

"She was trying to make sense of her life. She was trying to reconcile with her sister, but her sister kept rejecting her. She had allied herself to the Colonel, but the Colonel had decided to leave her. She felt called to do something, but she wasn't sure what. She only knew—or at least, she believed—that Edmund's walking-on-water picture was some kind of challenge. I think she felt . . . Look, I was thinking the other day that most of us like being useful. For most people, that doesn't mean much more than holding the door open for the next person, running an errand for someone who's too old or too sick to do it themselves, maybe volunteering for a charity from time to time. For Hilary, being useful meant sending people to a better place."

"But why pretend to be Edmund?" Dr. Muriel said.

"To outwit him. To show that she was better than him. She was always following other people. Always copying their blueprint for a better life. She wanted to take Edmund's trick and use it against him."

They watched Hilary, out at sea, still paddling.

"It is odd," said Tim. "The way her cloak hangs straight down like that. Has she got something in the pockets?"

"What about the late-night walk?" Chris prompted. "Last night, with Madame Nova, while we were in Edmund's room for the séance."

From the bed, eyes closed, Madame Nova said, "Wharrever I did, 'm sorry."

Emily reassured her. "It wasn't you. Hilary pushed Edmund's

body out to the top of the cliff in a wheelchair last night, dressed up to look like you, and she tipped him into the sea. After she'd got rid of the body, she wrapped herself up in your leopard-skin cloak and put on the sunglasses, wheeled herself back in through the basement and came up in the elevator. You were probably sparked out drunk, so Hilary could have come and gone without you noticing."

"Wasssn't drunk," said Madame Nova.

"How did Hilary get her into the bath this morning?" said Tim. "Took two men to get her out of there."

Emily pointed to the wheelchair. There was a sturdy room service menu and a wine menu stacked on the seat, both in hard-backed folders designed to withstand wear and tear from hungry, thirsty guests. "If she got her into the wheelchair, I'm thinking she maybe used those as a ramp so she was high enough to tip her into the bath. Or, I don't know, Hilary could have just told her to get in and then hit her over the head. She was pretty befuddled. Hilary probably gave her some sleeping pills mixed in with the drink."

Madame Nova protested again. "Not feeb . . . not beef . . . not beduddled."

Out at sea, with the lifeboat still more than half a mile away, Hilary was making an attempt to stand on the surfboard. She wobbled a bit, but she managed it, arms outstretched.

"Oh my goodness," said Sarah. "It looks . . . it looks as if . . ."

It looked as if she was walking on water. The surfboard lay on top of the water beneath her feet, but it was barely visible. The sun was low in the sky, climbing behind her. For a few moments, as she stood on the water, it bathed her in beautiful gold light.

Then she fell into the sea. She struggled. The coastguard's boat was too far away to reach her. She went under, then bobbed up again. Then she went under. She drowned.

Chapter Twenty-Seven
The Password

They went back down to the Riviera Lounge and had breakfast. What else could they do? The press were outside. The police were inside and would be wanting to interview them. Gerald still had a conference to run. They were hungry. Even Madame Nova insisted on joining them, having refused a ride to the hospital in an ambulance, and having received a begrudging all-clear from the paramedics who'd been called to attend her. She had dark glasses on. She was drinking coffee. She had bruises coming up that would rival Emily's. Only Joseph Seppardi was still in his room, tired out from the séance the night before. And yes, Mandy Miller had called up to check on him. He was all right.

The marbles were beginning to run clockwise. Gerald had his newspaper open, making an attempt at the cryptic crossword. Plates were piled high with sausages, egg and bacon. Talk turned to what people planned to do after they left Torquay.

Tim and Sarah would be going to Africa with Chris and the Colonel, setting up a foundation to bring safe water to people without access to it, combining digging boreholes with providing education through theater.

"In memory of Liam and Trina," said the Colonel. "Using water to bring blessings to people. Just, you know, in a different way."

"I thought our Liam brought us here to find other people to help," said Sarah. "And he did, in a way. But he wanted to help us, too. He wanted us to find friends." She flushed. "I know how it

214

sounds. But we were so lonely and lost. We didn't know what to do with ourselves back in Northampton, did we, Tim?"

Tim put his hand to the top of his head, patted his hair, found reassurance there. "I, uh. It's good to have someone to work with, you know? I can work with the Colonel."

"Colonel," asked Emily. "Why do people call you that? Were you ever in the military?"

"It's a nickname I picked up in university." He smiled, a little bashfully. "I was very fond of fried chicken."

In his way, the Colonel was as charismatic as Edmund Zenon had been, and as handsome—but with more humility. His eyes were as blue as the tiles in a swimming pool. There was humor and courage in his face. He had an orator's voice and a soldier's broad shoulders. It had been easy to believe he had led glorious campaigns overseas. There was nothing pious or pompous about him. Whatever you had done that you were ashamed of, he'd probably seen it or done it and beaten it. He was unshockable and nonjudgmental. He was the doctor you'd trust to tell you you were dying, he was the friend you'd trust to dig your grave. But there was no denying it: the revelation about his nickname diminished him slightly.

"And what language were you speaking, when Edmund was doing his trick by the pier? Was it an ancient curse?"

Dr. Muriel answered, chuckling. "He was speaking Welsh. *Dros ben llestri* means 'going over the top,' doesn't it? I don't know about the other one."

"*Chware'n troi'n chwerw*—is that what I said? It means 'play turns to spite,' as near as I can explain it. It's something you'll say to a group of children when they're too boisterous; you can see it's getting out of hand." The Colonel looked very sad. "Something I don't understand about Hilary. Why go to all the trouble of faking Edmund's death like that, and then just go paddling off into the sea?"

It was Madame Nova who answered. "She never could stick at anything. She's been an actress, an activist, a Hare Krishna. She's been one of those people who don't eat anything—whatever they're called, they get their nutrition from the air? Obviously that didn't last long. The search for meaning was the thread that ran through her life. She was eager to learn from other people, she was looking for a guru. At one time, she even considered herself an acolyte of Edmund Zenon— she bought his books, she went to his shows. I suppose, in the end, you could say she realized she was responsible for her own salvation."

"It's so awful that she took three people with her," said Sarah. "Really awful."

"As journeys of self-discovery go, it's not exactly *Eat, Pray, Love*, is it?" remarked Dr. Muriel.

"Why kill them?" said the Colonel. "We were supposed to be giving a new life to people. We were supposed to be helping people."

"I think she thought she was helping Trina," said Emily. "She was disposing of her, because she was no longer useful. But she did it by sending her to 'a better place.' She was frightened of Peg. She thought she had special powers and she might tune in and discover what Hilary had done. With Edmund, she was responding to a challenge she had seen in his walking-on-water picture, repeated in the bar when they made that wager that she could get him to walk into the water to get blessed. I think she thought she was doing that one for God."

The Colonel sighed, very deeply. There were tears in his blue eyes. "I'm ashamed I didn't see it and try to stop her. I thought she was good."

"Why did she go out there dressed in your clothes?" Gerald said to Madame Nova.

Madame Nova took off her glasses and rubbed the bridge of her nose. "Maybe it was her way of taking me with her. She was determined to have a reconciliation."

Tim's explanation was more prosaic. "I think the pockets in the cloak may have been concealing something heavy that helped her drown."

"Wine bottles, I expect," said Madame Nova, as if everyone carried wine bottles in the pockets of their clothes.

Gerald was still trying to get it all straight in his head. "You were trying to warn us with your predictions and your phone call?"

"I knew that if Hilary came to Torquay, it wouldn't end well."

"But how did you know she would come?"

A coffee-bitter smile. "It wasn't my psychic powers, if that's what you mean. She called me and told me she'd come. So I started my campaign. I wanted you to cancel the conference. I wanted Edmund to call off his challenge. I didn't even know about the trick he had planned. I saw the picture of a man standing on water and I thought, what happens next? And, of course, if he was an ordinary man, he would drown. I thought if I said it, other people would think that when they saw the poster, too, and they'd be frightened and join their voices with mine. But they didn't."

They sat in silence, thinking about Hilary. Like Edmund's walking-on-water picture, her death had a slightly different meaning for them all.

Then Dr. Muriel changed the subject. "How's your crossword going, Gerald? You seem to be getting on better with it than usual, today."

"I'm struggling with two down. Eight letters. The clue is: The unfunny brother gives a lesson in two acts on a rush hour defeat."

Dr. Muriel turned the newspaper so the crossword faced her. "The unfunny brother, I think, is Karl Marx."

Gerald picked up his pencil and turned the crossword back. "Two acts refers to that famous quote of his, then? History repeats itself. First as tragedy, then as farce."

Sarah said, "How odd. We had that last night. That's what Joseph said in the séance."

"That is odd," Dr. Muriel agreed.

"A rush hour defeat could be Waterloo station, couldn't it?" Emily suggested.

Dr. Muriel turned the paper back again. "Eight letters. I think the answer's Napoleon. That quote from Marx was about Napoleon Bonaparte and his useless nephew, also called Napoleon. The former—the famous one—was of course defeated at Waterloo."

"Napoleon? But it can't be!" Gerald looked as if . . . well, he looked as if he'd seen a ghost. "Well, blow me down," he said.

Dr. Muriel spoke patiently. "What is it, Gerald?"

"Nothing."

"You sound as if Napoleon is some kind of secret password." As soon as Dr. Muriel said it, she and Emily looked at each other, struck by the same thought: Lady Lacey Carmichael. Hadn't she given, and asked for, a password? They could see from Gerald's face that they were right. Napoleon was Lady Lacey's password. So what did it mean if Joseph Seppardi had sort of, almost, come up with it last night?

Gerald said, "I don't think Joseph's interested in Edmund's fifty thousand pounds."

Sarah hadn't been in the Ballroom and didn't know about Lady Lacey Carmichael and the secret password. She didn't know that Joseph might have been eligible for the money based on his performance last night, if Edmund weren't already dead. But she wanted to vouch for her friend. "He only cares about helping people."

Emily got out her notebook and looked over the notes from last night's séance.

A lady in lace had connected with Joseph. She had shown him a car. Michael. A husband. Brothers. Lady Lacey Carmichael, who had lost her husband and brothers in the war.

"About that," said Madame Nova.

About what?

Madame Nova opened her handbag and took a piece of paper from it. It was Edmund's cheque, made out to Hilary. "She left it in the room upstairs. What do you want me to do with it? Should I tear it up?"

Tim said, "Well, I'm not sure of the legalities. But wouldn't it pass to you as her nearest relative?"

"Fifty thousand pounds. That's a lot of money." Madame Nova looked from the Colonel to Chris, from Sarah to Tim—all of them trying to look virtuous, hoping she would choose to donate to their cause. "That would buy a lot of wigs." Madame Nova put the cheque in her handbag. She closed the clasp on it, firmly.

Gerald looked over at Emily. "Thank you for agreeing to come down here to make the report for our trustees. Without your observations and deductions, I'm not sure we'd ever have known exactly what happened. I'm just sorry you'll be back to your old job on Tuesday."

But Emily wasn't sorry. She was rather looking forward to it.

ACKNOWLEDGMENTS

Thanks to Terry Goodman, Anh Schluep, David Downing, Jon Ford, Sarah Rodriguez Pratt, Jacque Ben-Zekry, Danielle Marshall, Gracie Doyle and everyone at Thomas & Mercer who has been involved in the publication of this book, from design and production to editorial, marketing and publicity. There are so many people who have worked hard to make this book a success. Thanks to every one of you.

Thanks to my agent, David Hale Smith. I'm glad you're on my side.

My daughter, Lauren, read the manuscript and gave me notes on it. I borrowed her dimples and her sweet nature for the character of Emily in the book. I love you, Lauren.

Last year I went to CrimeFest in Bristol and Bouchercon in Albany, and I enjoyed them both very much. I'd like to thank the organizers for inviting me to take part in these events. If I had known that crime-writing conventions could be so much fun, I would have started writing crime fiction years ago.

I have had a lot of support over the years from reviewers and book bloggers. To everyone who has been kind enough to review one of my books, including this one, thank you.

And thanks to you for reading *Beyond Belief*. I'm proud of this book and it means a lot to me that you have taken the time to read it. I hope you enjoyed it.

ABOUT THE AUTHOR

British novelist Helen Smith's previous titles include *Alison Wonderland*, *Being Light* and *The Miracle Inspector*, as well as the Emily Castles mystery series. She lives in London.